*A
Harlequin
Romance*

OTHER
Harlequin Romances
by DOROTHY CORK

Many of these titles are available at your local bookseller,
or through the Harlequin Reader Service.

For a free catalogue listing all available Harlequin Romances,
send your name and address to:

HARLEQUIN READER SERVICE,
M.P.O. Box 707, Niagara Falls, N.Y. 14302
Canadian address: Stratford, Ontario, Canada.

or use order coupon at back of book.

A PROMISE TO KEEP

by

DOROTHY CORK

HARLEQUIN BOOKS

TORONTO
WINNIPEG

Original hard cover edition published in 1974
by Mills & Boon Limited.

© Dorothy Cork 1974

SBN 373-01812-6

Harlequin edition published September 1974

The Harlequin trade mark, consisting of the word
HARLEQUIN and the portrayal of a Harlequin, is registered
in the United States Patent Office and in the Canada Trade
Marks Office.

CHAPTER ONE

THE car broke down on a long hill road that wound through a forest where tall straight trees soared up against a cloudlessly blue summer sky. The sudden cessation of movement made the heat more intense, and Guy swore softly under his breath. Poor Guy, thought Lesley — he had been so good and uncomplaining about driving her all this way! He got out of the car to take a look under the bonnet, slamming the door shut behind him, and at the sharp sound, a flock of brightly coloured parrots rose screeching into the air before settling again.

Lesley with a sigh climbed out too, to stretch her legs and rouse herself from the torpor into which she had fallen during the long, long drive from Sydney. She had scarcely slept during the plane trip from England, and everything had a curious air of unreality, increased no doubt by the fact that she had left London in winter, and less than forty-eight hours later was suddenly sweltering in the Australian summer. The narrow apricot-coloured ribbon that tied back the ash-blonde hair from her neck had slipped, and she retied it as she made for the shade of the trees.

There was no point in her offering to help Guy. She knew nothing at all about motors, and she suspected that he didn't know much more, and she leaned against a tree trunk and watched him with an odd dispassionateness – odd, because she had come all these thousands of miles to marry him. They had not seen each other for two years, and the tanned, much-matured twenty-eight-year-old man, moustached and with unfamiliarly long red-brown hair, who had met her only this morning at the Sydney airport seemed to be almost another person from the man she had promised to marry back in England. She had been only nineteen then, and she wondered if Guy found her as much of a stranger as she found him.

The way things had happened, they had not even broached such a personal subject yet, and there had been no time to talk about the plans they had made so long ago. 'We'll be married as soon as you come out.' *Then*, they had both imagined Lesley would be here in less than a year. The doctors had given her grandmother one more year of life at the most, but she had managed nearly two, and Lesley had stayed with her.

The wonder was that Guy had waited for her. Two years ago he had not been so patient. He had been far too eager to start the adventure they had planned in a new country to wait for Lesley then, and he had gone ahead on his own, leaving her with a sapphire ring and assurances that he would have a job and a home, and a life waiting for her the minute she was free.

Well, he had the job – a good one in the accounts department of an advertising agency – and he was paying off the harbourside apartment he was living in at Kirribilli. As for their life together, their marriage, that must be talked about another day. Just now, they were making for Balgola on the far south coast of New South Wales on a mission that was still so completely unreal to Lesley that she had not yet even been able to weep ...

Guy slammed down the bonnet with a bang that caused another commotion amongst the parrots. Lesley asked sympathetically, 'Have you found the trouble, Guy?'

'Afraid not, honey. I haven't a clue what's gone wrong. She's packed up, that's all I know. I'll have to find a phone and get a mechanic to come out.' He joined her in the shade of the tall eucalypts. 'I'm sorry about this, Lesley. Life must seem just one ordeal after another to you since you stepped off that plane ... We've another twenty miles or so to Balgola Bay, and what I suggest is that you sit in the car while I walk back to the little dairy farm we passed two or three miles back. I'll phone through to the nearest town and see if I can get someone out to get the car going again. It looks like it'll be a couple of hours at least before we get you to the hospital, I'm afraid.' He put a finger under her chin and tilted her face up to his. 'It's been a gloomy reunion for us, hasn't it? And now this— What must you think of me?'

'It's not your fault,' Lesley said with a fleeting smile. 'It could happen to anyone.'

'Not if they'd had their car checked. And let's face it, I've been putting it off. Well, I'll be as quick as I can, honey. You won't be afraid all by yourself in the bush, will you? You look too done in to trudge miles in the sun.'

'I'll be perfectly all right,' she assured him. 'I'm only sorry *you* have to do it.' He kissed her briefly and she watched him go, thankful that at least it was a downhill walk, and then she went to sit in the car to wait. She felt guilty despite Guy's apologies. She shouldn't have let him drive her down today. She should have waited and caught the plane tomorrow. But it had seemed important to get to the hospital as soon as possible – to check with Dr. Garrison that Jane was going to be all right – to let them know there that she would look after her little niece as soon as she was ready to be discharged. Guy, as a matter of fact, couldn't have been more co-operative. Of course you must go,' he had said. 'It will be no trouble – I've more or less arranged to take the day off in any case.'

That had been this morning at his flat where he had brought her from the airport. He had arranged for her to stay for her first week at any rate in an adjacent apartment belonging to a girl called Emma, who was away on holiday, but they had gone into his flat first. And there he had broken the news to her that her sister Linda and her brother-in-law Tony Jarmyn had drowned just over a week ago. It was shocking news, and Lesley, who had been all too aware of something strained in his manner, had wondered if he was going to tell her he had fallen in love with another girl!

'There was no point in cabling you in London,' Guy

had said. 'You had enough to contend with, settling your grandmother's affairs and arranging your flight, and I didn't want you upset while you were all on your own.'

It had been a shattering and unbelievable blow to Lesley, though she had seen next to nothing of Linda, her senior by nine years, since she had married Tony Jarmyn, an Australian, over three years before. Tony and Linda had gone to Australia before Jane was born – now she was going on for two – and Lesley had hoped that when he went Guy would see something of them, but apart from one or two encounters he had not done so. The last time Lesley had heard from Linda had been a couple of months earlier when her sister had written a tell-nothing letter from another new address, full of chatter about Jane's doings and progress – and with an odd little postscript that had puzzled Lesley ever since. 'Promise to help me when you come out, Lesley. *Promise*.'

Help her how? Lesley had wondered. With the child? In the house? Financially? Personally? ... She had replied to the letter at once, promising that she would help – she, the younger sister, the naïve girl of whom Tony had said when she had announced her engagement, 'You're too young and immature to know what love's all about. Heaven help Guy Longden – sooner him than me!' And here she was now, offering herself to her elder sister to lean on as her grandmother had leaned on her – 'My Lesley, my little true and loving Lesley whose strength is her purity.' Those words were almost the last that Grandmother Brooke ever uttered . . .

And now Linda herself had passed beyond help. The only thing Lesley could do for her now was to look after the small orphaned child she had left. And that was a task she would accept gladly.

Her reverie was broken by the squeal of brakes as a car drew up alongside Guy's Holden. Lesley's heart leapt. It was Guy back with help already! But she realized instantly that she was mistaken. The man in the yellow sports car was alone, and he was leaning out to call across to her in an Australian drawl, 'Are you okay there? Anything I can do to help?'

'Not unless you're a mechanic,' said Lesley with a smile.

He switched off the motor and climbed out of his car, and Lesley thought, 'Don't tell me he *is* a mechanic!' and she wished that Guy had waited. He was twenty-two or so with longish dark curly hair, and he was tall – thin and rangy, with dark brown eyes that had a slightly wicked look about them. He wore smart-looking jeans and an obviously expensive batik shirt open at the neck. He leaned down and looked in at Lesley, and smiled lazily.

'Bad news – I'm no mechanic, I'm an Arts student. Broken down, have you?'

'Yes. My fiancé's gone to get help,' said Lesley, colouring slightly under his frankly admiring gaze. 'He shouldn't be long.'

'Where are you going?'

'To Balgola Bay. Do you know it?'

'I sure do! My old man owns a pub there. I'm on my way home now.'

'Oh.' Lesley's mind was working rapidly. Guy had said two hours – supposing he were here now, wouldn't he suggest she take a lift with this university student while he waited for the mechanic? She glanced quickly at the face framed by the car window. Despite his wicked eyes, he looked the sort of person you could be friends with – *their* sort of person. 'Or *my* sort of person,' she corrected herself mentally, for these days she didn't know any of the people Guy mixed with. She hadn't met his flatmate Douglas Potter, and she hadn't met Emma from the next flat where she had been supposed to stay. She said slowly, 'I wonder—' and stopped.

'You wonder what? My name's Bob Prescott, by the way, and you're—?'

'Lesley Brooke.' She made up her mind quickly. 'I was wondering if you could give me a lift. I'm going to the hospital, you see, and—'

'Sure I can give you a lift,' he said with alacrity. 'What about your fiancé?'

'I'll leave him a note,' decided Lesley. 'I can lock the car from inside.' She opened her handbag and pulled out a small notebook and pen and scribbled quickly, 'Dear Guy, please don't be worried – I've accepted a lift with Bob Prescott whose father owns a hotel at Balgola Bay. I'll see you at the hospital later. Love, Lesley.'

A couple of minutes later she was sitting beside Bob and they were zooming down the coast. Lesley's hair flew back behind her like a silver banner, and a little of her tiredness dropped away.

'Couldn't be that you're going to nurse at the hospital,' said Bob after a short time. 'Nurses don't come as young or as pretty as you are – in my experience.'

'Thank you,' said Lesley, 'but I'm almost twenty-one and I'm not all that pretty. I'm not a nurse, though. I'm going to see my little niece. She was in an accident – her – her parents were drowned when their car went into a flooded river—'

For the first time that day, tears came into her eyes and ran down her cheeks, and she cried silently for perhaps two minutes for her lost sister, and the young man beside her said nothing. He knew she was crying, for presently he put out a hand and touched her arm, slowing down as he did so.

'I'm sorry. Then it must have been your sister or your brother—'

'My sister,' said Lesley shakily. 'She was a lot older than me – and we hadn't seen each other much for years, but I'd been looking forward to – to—' She stopped, unable to go on.

'You poor kid. How old's the little girl?'

'She's going on for two – a baby still.' She glanced at Bob and saw that he was frowning.

'I remember that accident well,' he said after a moment. 'The parents escaped from the car before it went down and the little kid was washed out through

12

the window. A truck-driver saw her being carried along by the current and he grabbed her when she was close enough to the bank. The father was an artist of some sort, wasn't he? As a matter of fact, my old man—' His voice faded out and he said no more.

Lesley, who had heard no details of the accident – Guy had merely told her that Linda and Tony were driving to Melbourne and that their car had skidded on the wet road and gone into the river – felt her heart contract. She closed her eyes briefly, then opened them again. 'Your father—' she prompted.

'He identified the bodies,' he said soberly after a second. 'He knew the – Jarmyns, wasn't it? – because they'd stayed at the hotel several times . . . How is the baby? At least if she's a patient of Grenville Garrison's you can be sure she's having the best care available.'

'She is,' said Lesley. 'Guy said Dr. Garrison has a wonderful reputation.'

'True. Gren Garrison is one of those dedicated types who's opted out of life in any personal sense and is up to his eyebrows in his work. Very handsome eyebrows at that. Women go mad about him, but all he thinks of is the hospital and the kids who come in from hundreds of miles around. He's acquired a house on the property next door to the hospital so that mothers can stay there and be near their children. All very philanthropical and noble . . . However, as you're not a mother, Leura House won't be of any great interest to you.'

'It could be,' said Lesley, who had been listening with interest. 'I shall stay awhile – and of course I shall take Jane when she leaves the hospital.'

Bob whistled. 'Girl, you don't know what's ahead of you! Believe me, you're going to be well and truly vetted before ever that happens ... What sort of a bloke is this fiancé of yours? Is he all for taking on a two-year-old along with a bride? He'd better be, or you'll never in a lifetime get your tiny mitts on that baby.'

'Who will stop me?' asked Lesley, nettled. 'She's my niece – I should think I have a right to her.'

'Not unless it's in the best interests of the child,' said Bob. 'Grenville Garrison's going to want to know all about you and your prospective husband, so you'd better make it a good story.' He braked and Lesley became aware that they had come within sight of the glinting sapphire blue sea once more. Down below, spreading from a sparkling white beach back to the long slopes of bush and tree-covered hills, was the sprawl of a large and thriving town. At the far side of the bay on a low headland stood a three-storied building of light brick and stone, facing the sea and a row of tall Norfolk Island pines. Beyond in a garden, Lesley could see a large white bungalow.

'Balgola Bay,' said Bob. 'The hospital – and Leura House.'

Soon they were driving through the town, and then they reached the road that ran by the beach. Bob pointed out the Pacific Hotel, and Lesley glimpsed great tubs spilling over with flowers, striped canvas blinds shading balconies, a table-dotted terrace that

14

looked on to the sea.

'That's ours,' said Bob. 'Come in any time you like.'

At the hospital, he drove through the wide gateway and let Lesley out under a covered portico, coming round to open the door for her. He took her hand as she stepped out and smiled down into her eyes.

'Do I see you again?'

Lesley looked back at him. He was nice but – yes, his eyes were definitely wicked. She shook her head firmly. 'I don't think so. But thank you very much for the lift, Bob.'

He smiled ruefully. 'It was a pleasure.' He still had hold of her hand, and he pulled her suddenly towards him and kissed her squarely on the lips. 'I'll be around if you change your mind! 'Bye for now.'

Taken very much by surprise, Lesley was left speechless. She stood for a moment watching him drive off before she turned to mount the steps to the hospital entrance. The little incident with Bob vanished quickly from her mind as she remembered what he had said about her chances of looking after Jane. Of course she was going to adopt her own niece! Surely it was nothing to do with Dr. Garrison. She was certainly not going to have him question her about Guy. In her heart she knew very well that she and Guy would not have rushed into immediate marriage even if this business of Jane had not come up. The two years just gone had set them apart and it was yet to be discovered how well the breach would heal . . .

Inside, the girl at the inquiry desk gave her a sharp look when she said that her name was Lesley Brooke and that she had come to see her niece Jane Jarmyn.

'I'll ring straight through to Dr. Garrison,' she was told. 'He'll want to see you first.'

Lesley waited, and presently the girl turned back to her. 'Please take a seat. Dr Garrison will be down presently.'

Lesley thanked her. She sat down in a sunshine-coloured chair of moulded fibreglass, facing glass doors that looked out over the spectacular sapphire sea. The tall pines made dark vertical splashes against its singing colour, and a few white seagulls wheeled soundlessly. It was a beautiful situation for a hospital, and Lesley was sure that it would be no hardship at all to stay at Balgola Bay. Guy had holidays coming up – maybe he had been saving them with a honeymoon in mind, but maybe too he would have to use them so that he and Lesley could get to know each other again. What better place than here on the coast? They could swim – sunbathe – talk.

A few minutes passed, and then footsteps sounded softly but firmly on the rubberized floor. Lesley looked round quickly and got to her feet. Her heart began to hammer nervously. A tall broad-shouldered man in the immaculate white coat of a doctor came towards her. He had a lean suntanned face and thick black hair that showed a glint of silver at the temples. His eyes, very dark grey and blackly lashed, looked at her searchingly, and his smile of greeting was the merest formality, quickly gone. 'Am I being vetted already?' wondered Lesley, suddenly aware that she was in no condition to be scrutinized so thoroughly. She had not taken time off to tidy her hair after that drive in Bob Prescott's sports car, and she knew that her always pale face was now parchment white with exhaustion, and that there were dark shadows under her eyes. Weariness, nervous strain, always affected her that way, and she had had more than her fair share of those in the past twenty-four hours. Undeniably, Dr. Grenville Garrison was shatteringly handsome – she could hardly keep her eyes off him – but from the extreme coolness of his regard she could also well believe that he had opted out of life in the personal sense. It was at least a blessing to know that his reputation as a pediatrician was so excellent . . .

He held out his hand and took hers briefly, and she was aware of his quick glance at her sapphire ring. He spoke coldly. 'Good afternoon, Miss Burke. I'm Grenville Garrison. I'm in charge of your niece's case. I'd like to have a few words with you before you see her. Will you come along with me?'

'Thank you,' said Lesley. Her legs were shaky despite herself as she let him direct her across the lobby, and stepped ahead of him into a small intimate room that was half sitting-room, half office.

'Please sit down.'

She did so and he took a chair behind a narrow elegant desk that was graced by a large bowl of red roses whose perfume hung disturbingly on the air.

'Now, Miss Burke.'

Still his eyes refused to leave her alone, and Lesley, who wanted to protest at being called Miss Burke, somehow found herself unable to utter.

'First of all, is this merely a duty visit?'

The unexpectedness of the question, the cynical lift of the dark eyebrows that accompanied it, made Lesley blink. She felt almost as if she had been slapped, and she said indignantly, 'Of course it's not! Jane is my niece.'

'I'm aware of that,' he said dryly, 'but it's somewhat irrelevant.'

'Not at all,' said Lesley. Her smoky blue eyes locked with his, and she registered the indisputable fact that he was hostile. But why? – when they had only just met. 'Jane is my responsibility now.'

'Not necessarily.'

'But she is,' said Lesley, puzzled. 'And I'd like to see her – and I want to know how she is.'

'Yes, of course. You'll see her presently. As to how she is—' he leaned towards her, his eyes hard, 'Jane is a very sick little girl. She's been knocked about, she's badly shocked, badly bruised, badly concussed. We've been fighting for her life.'

Lesley felt the colour go from her face. She swallowed, her eyes wide. 'Will she get better?'

'I think so. But you understand concussion is a very tricky business, particularly when the patient is so small. Jane is going to need a lot of care, a lot of loving.'

Lesley said, her throat tight, 'I'm here now.'

He sat back in his chair and narrowed his eyes. He said with a chilling deliberation, 'Yes, you are here now. We must be grateful that you have managed to fit us into your social agendum, Miss Burke.'

'Miss Brooke,' Lesley breathed. 'Lesley Brooke.' Her heart was pounding at the unexpectedness of his attack. 'I – I don't—'

'I apologize,' he interrupted without waiting for her to finish speaking. 'Miss *Brooke* ... However, I don't imagine your – visit – here is going to work a miracle, grateful though we are to you for coming. Jane needs love, security, permanence, if she is to thrive. It's as simple as that ... Presently I shall take you to see her, and then you may return to your arduous life in the city with an easy conscience. As soon as it is practicable, I promise you I shall find someone with a loving heart to adopt and care for and cherish your niece.'

Lesley stared at him incredulously. What on earth was he talking about? And was he out of his mind or was she out of hers? Just how inhuman did he think she was, for heaven's sake? Out of her anger, she asked him that very question.

'Just what sort of a girl do you think I am, Dr. Garrison?'

His mouth twisted cynically, and those dark somehow mystical eyes explored her face once more.

'An exceedingly pretty girl,' he said at last. Lesley's colour rose furiously with the shock of those so lightly spoken – almost insulting – words, then subsided again leaving her white-cheeked. 'Even,' he continued clinically, 'a very charming girl. But – and you will have to forgive me for being frank, 'for you did ask me, you know – a very young and I would say a very irresponsible girl.'

'What a hopelessly stupid and unfair thing to say!' Lesley flared. 'After five minutes, how can you possibly know the least little thing about me? I'm practically twenty-one and I assure you that I'm far from irresponsible. You can forget about – about finding someone with a loving heart to care for Jane, because *I* am going to do that.'

'To find someone?' he suggested, with a tilt of his brows.

'No. I'm going to look after her – you must know that's what I meant.'

He said nothing for a moment. He gazed down at the bowl of red roses, idly drew out a bud and savoured its fragrance. Then his eyes met Lesley's once more and he said gently, 'You don't really mean that – not in your heart. You're over-reacting. Let's be quite logical and honest about this – it's a serious matter. You can't be expected to disrupt your life by taking a small child into it, and had I known you were so young I should never have considered it. At your age it's perfectly natural to be immersed in your own love life and all its delightful and frivolous deviations.'

'Oh!' gasped Lesley. 'I happen to be engaged to be married!'

His eyebrows lifted quizzically. 'I'm afraid I saw

your arrival at the hospital, Miss Brooke, so it's pointless to assume the role of virtuous, almost-married woman. That eye-catching orange dress of yours is unmistakable – and so is Bob Prescott's yellow sports car.'

Lesley stared at him speechlessly. Surely he was not judging her entirely on *that* little scene! The whole interview seemed to have gone crazy. It was like some fantastic and inescapable dream. She thought with sudden weariness, 'Why should I have to explain myself as if I were a naughty schoolgirl and this man my guardian?' But common sense reminded her that he was Jane's doctor – respected, reputable, dedicated. Bob Prescott had warned her that she would be well and truly vetted before she would be allowed to lay claim to Jane, but she still had not expected such opposition. It was infuriating and frustrating to be so misjudged, to have even her youthfulness counted against her. She said after a moment's silence, keeping her voice calm and reasonable, 'My fiancé was driving me here, Dr. Garrison. The car broke down some miles away and I was lucky enough to get a lift with Bob Prescott while Guy waited for someone to come out from the garage. I – I didn't want to get here too late.' There was no way of explaining away Bob's kiss, and she didn't try, but she somehow managed a smile. 'Please don't think badly of me. And please – I should like to see Jane now.'

He had listened to her courteously enough, but she didn't think he was over-impressed. Rising, he said briskly, 'Then come along.'

Dizziness almost overcame her as she got to her feet. She was over-tired and very close to tears. She put a hand on the desk to steady herself, and he said sardonically, 'You young people have too many late nights.' She felt his hand under her elbow and moved away abruptly.

Neither of them spoke as they went up in the lift.

When the doors slid open, she followed him along the corridor. A nurse in blue uniform hurried soft-footedly by with a quick glance of respect for the doctor. Lesley was conscious of the clean hospital smell, glimpsed through glass doors a Sister with her white veil. Then Dr. Garrison ushered her into a small room with a cot in it. Green blinds were drawn at the window, so that there was only a dim light in the room. A nurse turned towards them.

'This is Miss Brooke, the baby's aunt, nurse.'

The nurse smiled at Lesley, her eyes curious. She had a pretty fresh face, and she moved aside so that Lesley could see into the cot.

In a moment, Lesley was looking at Linda's child for the first time. Jane lay on her side, perfectly still. Her eyes were closed, and the lids had a heavy bluish look about them. Her face looked tiny and white, and tendrils of dark hair like Tony's showed under the bandage around her head. Her body made such a tiny hump beneath the soft pink blanket that Lesley, looking down at her silently, found her eyes were full of tears. She longed to take the child in her arms, to kiss her, to comfort and heal her.

A minute passed, then the man behind her said, 'Come.'

She looked up at him, but could scarcely see for tears. He directed her from the room and the hovering nurse went back to her position by the cot.

Lesley said huskily, 'Does she lie like that all the time – not moving, not opening her eyes?'

They were back in the elevator, and she wiped her tears away. He told her coldly, 'Upsetting yourself is going to do nobody any good. There's every chance that she'll make a complete recovery. But I've seen too many of these cases to make you a promise. She could open her eyes tomorrow – even tonight.'

'And then?' breathed Lesley.

'Then she'll need careful watching to make sure there aren't any complications.'

'I'll be here,' said Lesley. 'I'll be here.'

'The nurses will be here,' he corrected her sceptically. 'You've made your gesture, Miss Brooke. Don't take it too far, don't be carried away by sentimentality. Have your cry out and then do a little hard thinking. The child must come first, and Jane will be better off with someone who really wants her.'

Lesley said nothing. Her throat was too constricted for speech. But she thought she hated Grenville Garrison more than a little for his hardness. He had no heart. She was convinced of that. The marvel was that he was so dedicated, so devoted to his work as a pediatrician. She wondered if he trampled over the feelings of young mothers the way he was trampling over hers. Surely they must cry too, to see their little ones sick or in pain ... All she could do was to show him how wrong he was about her – to be dignified, not to argue or protest or fly into a temper, but go quietly on in her own way. Maybe it would be hard – maybe downright unpleasant, but she was going to do it.

The elevator reached the ground floor, the doors opened and Lesley stepped out into the foyer. Firmly she was led in the direction of the door. Her 'visit' was over. She could go back to her love life – and its frivolous deviations. Or so *he* thought. But Lesley thought quite otherwise. She was not going to be intimidated or pushed around, particularly when she did not deserve such treatment.

They reached the big glass doors, and Lesley could see that the sun was going down. The darkness of the pine trees was enriched with glowing red, and the jewel brilliance of the sea was fading rapidly to the muted grey-pink of milky opals. Magpies warbled and gulls were crying, and there was a sadness mixed with the beauty of the scene.

'Well,' said the man beside her, 'shall we say good-bye and wish each other long life?'

Lesley raised her eyes and looked back at him steadily.

'No,' she said quietly. 'I'm staying at Balgola Bay, Dr. Garrison. I shall be back to see Jane tomorrow and tomorrow and tomorrow, and for as long as she needs me. I – I'm very grateful for the care you've given her,

24

and now that I'm here I hope I shall be able to help her too, and that she'll be happy to come to me when she's well again. Her mother, after all, was my sister.'

'Yes,' he said briefly. He looked at her for a long moment and there was an odd expression in his eyes. He said frowningly, 'Do I have to spell it out to you that having a two-year-old child on your hands will sadly diminish your good times?'

Lesley smiled a trifle wryly. She hadn't had what he meant by 'good times' for a long while. She had had too much responsibility in looking after her grandmother, while the man to whom she was engaged was thousands of miles away. Yet she would do it all again if she had to choose. To see her grandmother happy and contented and loved was worth ten times the sacrifice – if sacrifice it must be called. She would feel the same way about Jane. But it was plain that to argue with the dictums of this – this man in authority, this handsome hostile man – would get her nowhere. And she didn't intend to indulge in a recital of her life story. She said simply, 'You don't need to spell anything out to me. I may be young, but I'm not so young that I can't read for myself. Thank you for your advice – and for your warning. But I know what I'm about and I know what I want.' She paused. 'I want Jane.'

He regarded her intently, still frowning.

'When are you to be married, Miss Brooke?'

The question took her by surprise, and she answered quickly, nervously, 'Soon.' How true was that? she wondered guiltily. Until this morning, when she had met Guy again, she had believed it to be true. Now she didn't know at all. Reality, she had discovered, is a thousand miles apart from dream – from memory . . .

'Your fiancé will agree to take the child into his care?' He spoke sceptically, and disbelief was plain in his voice. This was not vetting, she thought rebelliously. This was prejudice – unfounded prejudice. And though she had no idea whether Guy would agree or not – or even whether his agreement was relevant – she uttered a firm and decisive 'Yes'. And at that moment she saw Guy himself drive through the hospital gates. Her heart leapt, and she knew instinctively that he must not be allowed to talk to Grenville Garrison yet. She said hastily, 'Thank you very much for your *civility*, Dr. Garrison, and for the interview. I'll see you tomorrow.'

In a flash she was through the door and running down the drive to meet Guy.

'What on earth's happened?' he asked as he reached across to open the door for her. He sounded vaguely alarmed, and she made herself calm down, smile at him, and say, 'Nothing. I was just coming and – I didn't want you wasting your time. I know you want to get back to Sydney.'

'I'm afraid I shall have to,' he agreed. 'I shan't get much sleep tonight as it is . . . What's the score with Jane? All those cuts and bruises mending nicely?'

'It's rather more than cuts and bruises,' said Lesley. 'Jane's not on the mend yet – she's still unconscious. She needs someone to stand by her. Linda would want it to be me.'

'I suppose she would,' he agreed gently after a moment, and added, 'You have a heart so soft, honey, it would put an angel to shame ... I feel a heel not to offer to stay with you, but I can't take my holidays right now. I have a deal to put over in the next couple of weeks – a new account I'm hoping to land. If I bring it off it could mean just the promotion I'm aiming for.' He was driving slowly down the road that led back to the town as he spoke.

'I have a sort of deal to bring off too, so I must stay here,' said Lesley wryly. 'We're a fine pair, aren't we? If I want to lay claim to Jane, I must be around to make it apparent. The pediatrician is a kind of bogeyman. He has me terrified.'

Guy said nothing for a moment. Then – 'You really want to lay claim to Jane, do you, Lesley?'

'Yes.' She glanced at his profile and found it almost frighteningly unfamiliar. 'Do you – mind, Guy?'

If she had thought his answer would tell her what his feelings for her were, she was wrong. He completely avoided the implications of her question and said, 'Well, honey, if it's important to you, you must stay. We've been apart so long now that a little longer isn't going to make any difference.'

'And you do have holidays coming up,' said Lesley, struggling against a feeling that they were worlds apart – mentally, if not physically.

'Yes. We can surely do something with those.'

They left the subject there.

27

Half-way down the hill, she remembered something Bob Prescott had told her and asked Guy not to take her to a hotel but to turn back. 'There's a place next door to the hospital where I can stay – Leura House. It's especially for the relatives of children who are hospitalized.'

And Dr. Garrison, she finished to herself, did not even mention it to her!

CHAPTER TWO

Guy took her as far as the gateway in the fence that enclosed the rambling homely garden of Leura House. Lesley insisted that he must not wait – he had a long way to go.

'I hate doing this,' he told her, his hazel eyes apologetic. 'Keep in touch, honey – and look after yourself.' He kissed her – in a brotherly way, she reflected – and got back into the car. She watched him drive off, then picked up her two suitcases and began to make her way determinedly through the garden towards the sprawling white timber bungalow.

The light was fading quickly, but a few magpies still flew about in the pines, and their sweet warbling notes carried clearly on the light sea breeze. Lesley could hear the whisper of surf on sand as she went through the garden where huge red hibiscus flowers glowed luminously in the dusk and the scent of red roses hung almost tangibly on the air, reminding her vividly of the bowl of flowers on Grenville Garrison's desk. Lights were shining from the bungalow and she climbed four steps on to a wide verandah floored with smoothly polished hardwood, and heard a baby's cry – a healthy lusty yell, not the wail of a sick child. She knocked at the open door, and a woman's voice called casually, pleasantly, 'Is that you, Gren? If you want me you'll have to come through. I'm busy in the kitchen.'

A little disconcerted, Lesley hesitated. She had expected something more formal, more like a guest house or a private hotel than this. 'Gren', the voice had said, and that most positively must mean Grenville Garrison. She wondered uneasily if he were expected, and she hoped very much that he was not. She had no desire to encounter him again any sooner than was necessary.

She began to walk down the hall. It seemed the best thing to do. The floor was of dark blue satiny vinyl, very clean and modern-looking, yet despite it, the house had a comfortable slightly old-fashioned air. Framed flower prints and a big oval mirror in an ornate but tarnished gilt frame adorned the walls, and an empty cane perambulator stood across one doorway. The baby's crying had ceased, and Lesley found herself at the door of a large kitchen. She was confronted by a surprised-looking woman – smallish, neat, in white starched veil and pale blue overall. Her unremarkable face was lightly suntanned and unpowdered, her nose was slightly turned up, her eyes were blue and as pleasant as her voice. She was fiftyish and she held a small baby against her shoulder.

'My goodness, who have we here?' she asked Lesley goodhumouredly. 'Someone I haven't been told about.'

Behind her, in a battered high chair, a small pyjamaed child, his face smeared with egg yolk, banged a spoon and shouted, managing at the same time to upset a mug of milk on the floor. Diverted by this, he ceased his other activities to watch the spreading flow of milk with a look of surprised delight. Lesley smiled a little and so did the woman with a baby.

Lesley opened her mouth to say – she was not certain exactly what she was going to say. But she had said exactly nothing when the necessity to explain herself was gone. A male voice behind her said, 'This is Miss Burke, Gilly. Or at least, it appears that her name is Miss Brooke. She arrived unexpectedly today.'

Lesley turned reluctantly, her cheeks stained with deep colour, her heart sinking. Dr. Garrison! It seemed she could hardly move without his being aware of it. What was he going to do now? Tell her that she could not stay here? But he merely gave her a rather grave smile, and added, 'This is Sister Gilbert, Miss Brooke.'

'Miss Brooke would not be coming at all, I seem to remember you saying,' remarked Sister Gilbert a trifle acidly. 'But she's come today, which shows that you never can tell. And she's ready to drop with fatigue by the look of her. Or haven't you noticed that?' Her expression indicated that the doctor was beyond hope, and Lesley, embarrassed, tried to pretend not to notice it. 'Sit down, Miss Brooke.' She indicated a shabby comfortable armchair by a door that led to a verandah. 'Dear me, I can't call a young girl like you Miss Brooke. What's your first name, dear?' Her blue eyes looked at Lesley kindly, a little anxiously, and suddenly Lesley felt something inside herself relax. Here was a friend, she was sure – somebody to like and to trust.

She sank into the armchair, suddenly aware that she needed its support.

'My name's Lesley.'

'It suits you. I always think of Lesley as a blonde name somehow. I'm Mary Gilbert, but everyone calls me Gilly. I'll make you a cup of tea, Lesley, that will set you up. You'll want one too, I suppose, Gren.'

'No, thank you. I didn't call in to be sociable.'

'Then what did you call in for?' Gilly wondered. She handed the baby down to Lesley. 'Hold Deedee for me, will you, dear, while I clear up this mess that Rory's made. And tell me what it is that's made you so tired.' She reached for a cloth and stooped to wipe up the spilled milk, while Rory beat a soft tattoo with his bare feet and craned his small neck to watch her. Lesley, smothering a yawn, held the warm little bundle of a baby against her. She was acutely aware of Grenville Garrison standing, tall and impatient, just inside the doorway, and she knew he was watching her. She wondered what he was thinking and why he hadn't – denounced her, she thought ridiculously, as soon as he had followed her into the house. For she was certain he had seen her coming and had followed her.

She answered Sister Gilbert's question minimally.

'I've had a long day. A lot of things have happened.'

'Including,' said the small woman, straightening and looking accusingly at the doctor, 'a regular inquisition, I'll be bound. I hope you've conceded the poor girl the privilege of taking an interest in that little orphaned scrap at the hospital, Grenville. With a face like hers, I shouldn't suppose you'd need to think twice.'

His dark eyebrows lifted. 'Come now, you don't expect me to hand the child over unquestioningly to the first person who turns up, relative or not.'

Sister Gilbert, putting the kettle on to boil, ignored this, and Lesley felt somewhat bewildered. Her impression of Grenville Garrison as a heartless, single-minded 'bogey', as she had called him to Guy, seemed to be dissolving before her eyes. This woman must surely have known him for a long time to treat him so casually – and to treat him as the most human of men. Lesley almost felt that she should not be there, that Dr. Garrison would be furiously angry at this destruction of the image of a man in authority, a man not to be questioned, not to be defied. Well, she, Lesley, had defied him already. She had stayed when he had said 'Go'. And now Sister Gilbert turned to ask him, 'And how long is Lesley to stay with me?'

'I'm not sure that she's to stay at all,' he said. 'I didn't send her here, you know. She somehow or other found her own way.'

His eyes looked at Lesley speculatively, and she said with a touch of defiance, 'Bob Prescott told me about Leura House. I thought that anyone could stay here if they had a – a child in the hospital.'

'And of course you're to stay,' said Sister Gilbert with an indignant look in Dr. Garrison's direction. 'Your being here could make all the difference to that

33

baby. Love is a child's greatest need.'

'A love that's constant,' said Grenville Garrison chillingly. 'Not a love that's handed out on some momentary impulse and then withdrawn.'

Lesley flushed angrily. 'My love is not given like that. Jane is my niece – my sister's child.'

'And because of that, you expect me to believe that you love her almost maternally?' he asked cynically.

'Yes,' said Lesley. Her eyes were caught and held by his and there was an oddly charged silence in the room until Sister Gilbert, who had been watching them curiously, broke the spell.

'I'll take that baby in a moment, Lesley, just as soon as the tea's made. I shall be pleased when Tracy comes home to give her her feed,' she added, reaching for the kettle. 'How is Barbara today, Grenville?'

'Fine. Tracy can take her home in a few days.' He watched as Lesley handed the baby over.

'I'm glad to hear that. I can't say it's all beer and skittles managing these two at my age with all the multitudinous other things I have to accomplish.'

'You want it both ways, don't you, Gilly?' His smile was unexpectedly quizzical and kind – not in the least like the dry humourless smiles that had been all he had offered to Lesley. 'One minute you're telling me you can do any number of things at once without so much as turning a hair, and the next you're complaining about getting too old.'

Gilly ignored him. 'And little Sally Tressider?' she pursued.

'She's progressing. Her sleeping pulse rate's been normal for a week, and there's been no permanent cardiac damage done, I'm thankful to say. Once Jean has her home, I'll make it my business to get over to Merrigal every so often to check on her.'

'They don't have the best of luck, the Tressiders, do they?' Gilly gave Rory a rusk and another mug of milk, and with the baby tucked under her arm began pouring the tea. She explained to Lesley, including her in the conversation in a friendly way, 'Little Sally Tressider has had rheumatic fever. The Tressiders adopted her about eighteen months ago – she's five now – and in less than no time, Mrs. Tressider had died of a cerebral haemorrhage. I don't know why it should happen to someone like Ian. He's the rector at Merrigal and no man could have a bigger heart, not even Grenville here. His doors are open to everyone. His sister Jean's house-keeping for him now. She's an angel of mercy, but too old to mother a child of five.'

'She'll get by,' said the doctor dryly. 'She's not as old as all that.'

'Still and all, he should marry again,' Gilly insisted.

'You make it sound the easiest thing in the world,' said Grenville. 'You forget that in marriage – in love – human hearts are involved.'

Human hearts, thought Lesley. So he did admit that other people had hearts. *Other* people – but for some reason not her. *She* gave her love on impulse for a day or two.

'I don't forget,' said Sister Gilbert. 'But I have little patience with people who shut themselves away with a memory.'

His eyebrows went up but his mouth was grim, and there was a dangerous-looking glint in his eyes. He said briefly, 'Ian doesn't do that.'

'No – *Ian* doesn't,' Gilly agreed, and Lesley was aware that his unspoken warning did not intimidate her. It was heartening to find that he could not bluff everyone. Gilly's glance had grown piercing too, then suddenly it softened and she said lightly, 'While I think of it, Gren, there are one or two cheques in the office for you to sign. Have you time to attend to them?'

'I shall have to make time, shan't I?' His look too had softened, and was now wholly affectionate, and Lesley wondered if she had imagined that small flame of hostility that seemed to have flared up briefly between them. 'I have no doubt they're overdue, and if I don't make a point of it you'll have your creditors carrying away the furniture, high chairs, cots, perambulators and all.' He grinned suddenly, showing the whitest teeth Lesley had ever seen, though perhaps it was the contrast with his tanned face, and moved inside the house.

Gilly rocked the baby and helped herself to more tea.

'So you want to take little Jane Jarmyn after all,' she remarked. 'I'm glad you're to have a chance. I'm glad Grenville hasn't let his first impressions get the better of him.'

36

'First impressions?' repeated Lesley, puzzled. What could Sister Gilbert know of the doctor's first impressions of her? She couldn't possibly be referring to that silly kiss Bob Prescott had given her – she would need supernatural powers to know about that.

The older woman smiled at her apologetically. 'If you could have come sooner, Lesley, it would have been a strong point in your favour.'

Lesley blinked. Having stepped off the plane from England only that very morning, how on earth could she have come any sooner? She had begun to say, 'That just wasn't possible,' when Grenville reappeared.

'I'm going to take Miss Brooke off your hands in a minute, Gilly. I know you're not geared to provide meals for unexpected arrivals.'

That of course was a dig at Lesley for taking it upon herself to think she had a right to stay at Leura House. Apparently she hadn't. Apparently it was Dr. Garrison who said who was to stay and, conversely, who was not to stay. The very fact that he had not mentioned Leura House to Lesley told her plainly in what category *she* came.

Gilly said pleasantly, 'I may be careful with my funds, Grenville, but there's always enough to feed an extra mouth or two. For any meal. And no matter how big the appetite – as you should know yourself. A little resourcefulness can always overcome a slight shortage of meat and vegetables.'

He made a wry face and smiled slightly – a smile that was strictly for Gilly. Lesley knew that she was excluded, and hoped that she would be left in peace to eat her meal at Leura House and to go early to bed. The earlier the better.

But it was not to be.

'All right, you've won your point. Far be it from me to deny your resourcefulness. However' – he turned a frowning glance on Lesley – 'Miss Brooke and I still have things to discuss – since she's still here.'

'And you couldn't leave the poor girl in peace until tomorrow?' With the baby tucked under one arm she lifted a wriggling and replete Rory from the high chair and set him on his feet.

'I'm afraid I couldn't. I have a full morning in the theatre tomorrow. And my afternoon is not exactly free either.'

Gilly sighed. 'You do as you please, Lesley. You're a free agent – though some people are not aware of it ... There's Tracy now.' She gave Rory a pat on his little rump. 'Come on and we'll meet your mother.'

Dr. Garrison looked at Lesley and she could read nothing at all in the darkness of his eyes.

'Will you have dinner with me, Miss Brooke?' he asked almost formally.

Lesley longed to say no and to say it emphatically. But she had foisted herself on Sister Gilbert, and besides, if Dr. Garrison was determined to have a further discussion with her – which meant, she suspected, that he was going to give her another lecture, advise her once more to go away – then she might as well get it over. She would also do a little discussing herself, and put him straight as to why she had not come any sooner.

She said aloofly, 'Thank you. But if I may, I'd like to freshen up a little first.'

'Do that.' His eyes flicked over her. Critically? Lesley didn't know in the least what he was thinking. 'You'll find a bathroom two doors along.'

She found the bathroom. The mirror over the wash-basin showed her a pale face with dark shadows under smoke blue eyes that had a lost look about them. She did her best to camouflage the signs of weariness with make-up, combed her ashy blonde hair and retied the ribbon that held it back. Her sleeveless apricot dress was of a creaseless material, and she had discarded the jacket long ago. It was with her luggage that she had left in the hall. She supposed that she looked passable, but on second thoughts reflected that it didn't much matter anyhow; Grenville Garrison was not in the least interested in her appearance.

When she returned to the hallway, he was waiting for her just outside the front door. Her luggage had disappeared, lights shone from two partly open doors and she could hear a woman's voice that was not Gilly's coming from the direction of the kitchen. The mothers were evidently returning from the hospital, and suddenly the house was warmly alive.

She made her way towards that waiting male figure on the verandah, and as she drew hear he turned towards her.

'If you want anything from your luggage, it's in the

room at the end of the side verandah. It's a small room, but you'll have it to yourself.'

Lesley gave him a polite smile. 'Thank you. But I'm quite ready.'

'Good.' Then, carelessly, 'You shouldn't need a jacket. The night's warm, and I shan't keep you out late.'

'I'm sure you won't,' said Lesley coldly. She walked past him and down the verandah steps, her head held high. 'I'm sure that both of us want to get our – discussion – over as quickly as possible.' She rather wished the words back as soon as they were out of her mouth. It was not going to help to be rude, or to seem even less mature and responsible than he already thought her. A good impression was what she should concentrate on, if she had any sense.

But all the same, when she was sitting beside him in the darkness of the car and they were speeding towards the town by the bay, she could not resist saying, 'I could have eaten at Leura House, you know. I'm not in the least hungry.'

'Perhaps not. But since you've chosen to ignore my advice, either through contra-suggestibility or through the demands of a guilty conscience, you can dine with me while we get a few facts straightened out.'

She was relieved when he drove past the Pacific Hotel. It was obviously the sort of place where you could expect to get a good – and expensive – meal. Just the kind of place that Dr. Garrison would favour. Linda and Tony had patronized that particular hotel

40

too, she reminded herself – frequently enough for the proprietor to get to know them quite well. Had they stayed there, she wondered, or merely eaten there when they were passing through? How little she knew about Linda's life in Australia – except that almost every time she wrote it had been from a different address. Her last two or three letters had come from the same place – from Cremorne. And it was from Cremorne that Linda had written her odd little plea for help. Their trip to Melbourne could not have meant a move – not just around the time when Lesley was expected to arrive ...

She was aroused from thoughts that had drifted into a kind of waking dream by the realization that they had left the town behind them and that the car had come to a standstill outside a small lighted restaurant. Backed by silent bushland, it stood in the curve of a beach whose sand shone dazzlingly white in the moonlight. Lazy waves whispered in, dark and mysterious and laced with delicate white foam. Like drifting garlands of mayflowers in dark hair, she thought fancifully. The sky was full of stars, and the air was caressingly warm on her bare arms as she half climbed, half fell from the car, almost stumbling into Grenville Garrison's arms as he stood holding the door open for her.

It was a restaurant for lovers, was her first stupefied thought, as she preceded him inside. The notion shook her oddly. Small tables with rose red clothes, soft concealed lighting that showed a ceiling draped with flimsy fishing net and painted with mermaids frolicking in an opal sea; orange candles whose flames moved flickeringly in the movement of air that came through wide windows opened to the charm of a seductive silver shore, a murmuring sea, a pageant of stars in the heavens.

A pretty girl in a long sea green caftan showed them to a table, leading them past a low dais where a Chinese pianist played soft classical music that Lesley recognized with a vague pang of delight that was half sadness as being Mozart.

Her delight lasted only until she was seated at the table and the dark-faced man, silver glinting at his temples, seated himself opposite her. Unsmiling, unfriendly, business bent. No part of a weary, almost sensuous, dream.

A place for lovers? A place for a quiet inquisition . . .

He ordered John Dory and a side salad for them both without even glancing at the menu, and with merely a casual, 'I hope that will suit your palate?' to Lesley, who nodded her acceptance. She did not feel particularly interested in food in any case, and nothing seemed quite real. He named a specific white wine and asked for it to be brought to the table straight away while they waited for their dinner. He poured it himself into the stemmed wine glasses, and told Lesley briefly, 'Drink up – it will do you good.' She wondered tiredly if he brought many women here – his wife, maybe? – and then remembered he was supposed to have no personal life. That must mean no wife. But – no women friends? She glanced at him covertly as she sipped the wine. He was certainly too handsome for women to leave him alone, and despite the silver at his temples he looked a young and virile man, still in his thirties.

Opposite her, he sat back sipping his wine too and occasionally glancing at her. They could almost have been two more lovers amongst the rest, reflected Lesley. There were a dozen or more others in the small restaurant, most of them sitting at tables for two, not talking much but looking across the flickering candle flames into each other's eyes . . .

Dr. Garrison set down his glass and leaned towards her.

'Tell me about yourself, Miss Brooke,' he said abruptly. His eyes met hers and went briefly to her mouth.

Lesley bit her lip. She took another mouthful of wine and swallowed it nervously. She didn't know why she felt so disconcerted. She said uncertainly, 'I – I don't know what you mean – what you want to know.'

'I want to know what sort of a girl you are – apart from being somewhat sentimental and, I rather suspect, contra-suggestible. You're several years younger than your sister – Mrs. Jarmyn – was, aren't you?'

'Yes.'

'Well then – did you get on together? Did you see much of each other?'

'Not a great deal,' admitted Lesley slowly, hoping that this was not going to count against her. 'But we were very fond of each other. Our parents died eleven years ago, and my grandmother brought me up, but Linda was old enough to earn her own living and she went to London. I always thought she was – wonderful. Not because she was beautiful, not only that. She was kind too, she came home often, and she always brought fruit or flowers or something for our grandmother.' She broke off. She was not going to add to that, to admit to this man that marriage had made something of a stranger of Linda, that neither she nor her grandmother had liked Tony Jarmyn ... Fortunately their dinner arrived then, and they began to eat. The John Dory was delicious, but Lesley couldn't enjoy it and made little more than a pretence of eating. Presently she looked up to find his eyes on her, and for just a moment she thought their expression was not quite so analytical, or hostile – that there was a gleam of feeling there, perhaps of kindness. And then his lids and those heavy black lashes descended.

'Drink up your wine at least, Miss Brooke. It will help you to relax.'

Obediently she drank, and waited passively for him to go on.

After a slight pause he said, 'I've been giving some thought to Jane's case. Frankly, I didn't think you were interested in her – and certainly not in making her your responsibility.'

Lesley's eyebrows rose a little. 'You were wrong,' she said lightly.

He sent her a sceptical look. 'Initially, I was under the impression that neither of the Jarmyns had any

44

relatives in Australia – though I've since learned that Mr. Jarmyn has a brother in South Africa. As for you – as you've said, you were not close to your sister, and perhaps you have no stomach for tragedy.'

'That was certainly not why I—' Lesley began, but he interrupted without giving her a chance to finish, a fact for which she was later thankful. 'You may wonder how we were able to contact you, Miss Brooke. When the car was hauled up from the river a single page of a letter you'd written to your sister came to light – the last page. You may not recall it, but you'd written from wherever you were living at the time telling your sister that as of this month your address would be care of Guy Longden at Kirribilli.'

He looked at her steadily, and to her annoyance she flushed. He was so intent on seeing her in a bad light he was ready to believe anything of her. She would let him say all he had to say and then she would set him right, and she hoped he would apologize for all the wrong conclusions he had reached. She remembered very well the letter to which he referred. She had written it just after her grandmother's death, and she had given Linda Guy's address in a postscript because she knew the Jarmyns had not kept in touch with him. And because Linda had written, 'Help me'. She looked at the man opposite her and waited coolly for him to continue.

He told her accusingly, 'You were out dancing with your fiancé when I telephoned, Miss Brooke, and as

45

you know, I left a message with your fiancé's flatmate suggesting that you should come to Balgola Bay as soon as possible.'

Lesley was startled completely out of her tiredness. Her head whirled. How did all that add up? She had not even been in Australia when he had telephoned – she had certainly not been out dancing with Guy. And that meant that Guy had been out dancing with somebody else. But – his girl-friend! Regardless of how the knowledge affected her, it clearly would not do at all for Dr. Garrison to know the girl had not been her. Not if she hoped to present an image of an engaged and soon to be married girl, a girl who had all the necessary qualifications for becoming Jane Jarmyn's guardian ... She looked at him guardedly and waited to hear what else he had to say.

'I'll grant you that at least you rang back. I was given your little telephone speech verbatim – except that the telephonist somehow got your name wrong. Now, Miss Brooke' – he leaned towards her – 'you said that you would certainly come to see your niece. But that was a good week ago. Can you blame me for being somewhat sceptical as to the depth of your interest in Jane? Or can it be that you have such an important position to hold down that you couldn't be spared?'

Lesley shook her head. Her throat was dry. She said, 'I don't have a job—' and stopped.

'No job at present? What were you trained for, Miss Brooke?'

'I was training to become a nursery teacher, but I—'

'But you didn't complete your training.' His eyes said that he was not surprised. 'So no job. Then perhaps you were ill?'

He was handing her an excuse, but she couldn't take it. This girl-friend of Guy's, whoever she was, had put her in a very awkward spot. She couldn't tell the truth, so what reason could she give for having delayed coming to the hospital for a week? How could she possibly explain away the lack of interest that that implied? No wonder his first impression of her was bad! No wonder he was so doubtful about her sincerity in regard to Jane! Yet to tell him the truth could hardly improve her case. He would be at the least sceptical as to the likelihood of the success of her marriage.

Lesley was sceptical too. She wasn't altogether sure that she and Guy would ever marry. She had felt that way before she had learned of the existence of another girl – even though that girl might still prove to mean nothing in Guy's life. After all, he would have to be an extraordinary man not to have taken other girls out while he was waiting for Lesley. And yet – his 'girl-friend'! Guy's flatmate – Douglas Potter, in other words – had told Dr. Garrison that Guy was out dancing with his girl-friend – and at such a time!

She said huskily, 'I can't explain it just now. But I do care very much about Jane.' She found she was twisting her fingers around the stem of her wine glass nervously, and he reached across and took it from her.

47

'That glass will snap in a moment. It strikes me you need something to steady your nerves. Too many late nights. I'll tell Sister Gilbert to give you something. And while you're here – even if it's only for two or three days – I'd recommend a good dose of sunshine and a few early nights. A girl as young as you are should have colour in her cheeks.'

She looked across at him helplessly. He had ignored her remarks and she could only insist, 'I shall be here more than two or three days. Jane matters to me very much.'

He said nothing. He glanced away from her as if he would rather not see her and signalled to the waitress to bring the coffee. When it came, he offered her the sugar, then helped himself. She knew that she was looking wretched and guilty, and she suspected the fact pleased him. For her part, she wished she could go home – back to Leura House – and fall into bed and sleep for ever. Or at least for a good twelve hours. She had barely slept since leaving England, and she had had about as much tension as she could stand.

Certainly his next remark scarcely moved her – spoken while she drooped listlessly over the hot black coffee, and he leaned close to her. 'Take heed that for some idiotic reason you don't get yourselves too involved in this business before you decide to drop it. We don't want the child becoming attached to you only to find that she must lose you. There are plenty of good women who would like to adopt her.'

'There'll be no need for that,' said Lesley.

He gave her a hard look. 'Miss Brooke, are you aware that your brother-in-law left nothing?'

At that she sat up straight, her eyes flying wide open. She exclaimed incredulously, 'That can't be true! Tony was a clever commercial artist – he could always find work.'

'No doubt. One must also assume that he – and his wife – could spend money too. And did.'

So it had been financial help that Linda had needed, thought Lesley. Poor Linda!

'What is your fiancé's financial position?' the man opposite her asked bluntly.

'Guy is in advertising,' said Lesley. 'And in line for promotion. As a breadwinner, you can't possibly find fault with him.'

'As a breadwinner,' he repeated. 'It's regrettable he couldn't find time to come to the hospital today. I should have liked to talk to him.'

'It was late,' Lesley said quickly. 'We'd had a break-down. And he had to drive all the way back to Sydney.'

'I understand. Well, I shall see him when he comes this way again ... Is your wedding date set, by the way?'

Lesley coloured deeply. 'Not yet. But it's – under discussion.'

She was thankful that he asked for no more details. Those darkly compelling eyes made one more slow and detailed examination of her face in the flickering candlelight, and then abruptly, he said, 'Well, we shall see. And now if you've finished your coffee, I shall take you back to Sister Gilbert's ministrations.'

'Thank you,' said Lesley. She meant to say it with spirited sarcasm, but her voice came out subdued, exhausted. She had had enough, and he knew it, and strangely he was being merciful.

Less than half an hour later she was in bed. Gilly, no doubt on his instructions, had brought her a glass of warm milk laced with something, and a small white tablet, and her head had no sooner been laid on the smooth linen pillow than she could feel herself relaxing. In no time at all she was deeply, restfully, dreamlessly asleep.

CHAPTER THREE

SHE slept for more than twelve hours in the small verandah room that faced across the far side of the headland, below which was a small secluded beach. Lesley managed an occasional swim from that beach in the weeks that followed, but much of her time was spent at the hospital or helping Sister Gilbert at Leura House.

There was not very much yet that she could do for Jane, but she had the feeling that just by being there she could help, and she was determined that Dr. Garrison should know without any doubts at all that she took her role seriously. Tracy White introduced her to some of the women who were visiting their children, and on the whole she found them a friendly lot, with the exception of one, a Mrs. Nelson, who appeared to think her child's needs should take precedence over those of anyone else. Mothers were encouraged to visit particularly at mealtimes and at bedtime. Tracy White said that if Dr. Garrison could have his way, there would be living-in quarters at the hospital to accommodate mothers, and already plans were under way to raise money to build a separate children's block. Meanwhile, it was Grenville Garrison who had organized the facilities at Leura House. This caused Lesley to realize with some uneasiness just what she had done in taking it upon herself to go there. She wondered that he had let her stay.

Her second evening she telephoned Guy to tell him what she was doing and why she must stay.

'I'll come down for the week-end,' he promised. 'It will be great to see you again and have a real talk.'

It was a brief telephone conversation and an unsatisfactory one. Somehow it lacked depth, warmth. Once Lesley had recovered from the immediate shock of her sister's death, she had realized that the strained atmosphere between herself and Guy had some cause other than that of the tragedy. If she felt that he had changed, then it was likely he felt the same about her. She wondered if she had waited two years for a man who no longer existed, and now in addition there was the mystery of Miss Burke to be cleared up. She could hardly ask about *that* over the telephone, but she would certainly bring it into the open during the week-end – if only because it had put her in such an awkward position.

The following day for the first time she was allowed to watch Jane being fed nasally, and she found it distressing. The silence in the small darkened room, the utter absorption of the nurses, the complete helplessness of the tiny child with her pathetically bandaged head—

After a few minutes Lesley turned away and went into the corridor. Another time she would stay, but not this first time. And of course, Grenville Garrison *would* come along just as she was wiping away tears.

'What's the matter, Miss Brooke? Your little niece is doing fine.' He stopped and looked down at her quizzically, and Lesley put her handkerchief away and tried to avoid looking back into those compelling dark eyes.

'I know,' she said with dignity. 'It's just that – that I haven't seen a nasal feeding being given before.'

His eyebrows lifted. 'You'll get used to it if you persevere, I promise you ... Not going back to Sydney yet?'

'No.'

'I hope that man of yours will try to get down here again – it's important that I should talk to him.'

'For talk to, read vet,' thought Lesley, but she said quickly, 'He'll be here on Saturday.'

'Fine.'

After he had gone on his way she began to wonder nervously how she could handle the situation. It was not the normal one of an engaged couple who planned to marry soon. She and Guy hadn't yet got around to talking about themselves and their possible marriage, let alone the drastic step of adopting a two-year-old child. If he were taxed outright with the question unprepared, Lesley doubted very much whether he would back her up ...

On Friday, when she returned to Leura House for lunch, a little depressed by the apparent lack of change in Jane's condition, there was a message for her from Guy written on the notepad by the telephone in the hall.

53

'Lesley, Guy Longden rang. He won't be able to get down on Saturday after all – pressure of work,' Gilly had written in her firm upright script. 'If you take the Saturday afternoon plane to Sydney, he'll meet you at the airport.'

Lesley was aware firstly of a feeling of relief. That meeting between Guy and Grenville Garrison had really been worrying her. Now it was to be postponed and she would have a chance to talk to Guy, to reassess and to sort out their relationship.

She went to her little verandah room to tidy herself, to comb her hair. Her face in the mirror looked tired and dispirited. Well, everything would eventually be worked out. This week-end would surely bring about some sort of an advance in her relationship with Guy – she was determined on that. 'So cheer up, Lesley,' she thought, 'and remember that at least you can stand by that little mite in the hospital.'

She had managed to dispel her air of defeat when she went out to the kitchen. Gilly was talking to a dark-haired woman of forty or so whom she introduced as Jean Tressider, adding that she had come to take Sally home to Merrigal. Sally, a little round dumpling of a child with long fair hair, was outside playing in the yard. No one would ever think, to look at her, that she had been suffering from rheumatic fever. She wore red tights and a very brief yellow dress, and she was squatting on the grass watching a big blue and black butterfly.

'She's a sweetie,' said Lesley. 'I've talked to her a

couple of times in the ward. I'm glad to see her up and about.'

'So am I – though she *is* a handful,' Jean Tressider confessed. 'And not being her mother, I suppose I worry about her more than I should.'

Lesley went outside to say hello to Sally. She heard Gilly say, 'Ian should marry again. I hope he doesn't intend to nurse his heart for the rest of his life.'

'I don't think so. He's not as intense as Grenville.'

Lesley felt a strange tremor go through her. Grenville? Had he been married and lost his wife? That could account for the fact that he was so immersed in his work ... She talked to Sally for a little while and then Jean came out to collect the child, and Lesley went back inside.

Tracy was not yet back from the hospital. The baby, Deedee, was asleep and Rory was feeding himself messily in the high chair. Gilly was preparing a huge salad.

'Did you get your message?' she asked as Lesley sat down at the table to help her.

'Yes, thank you. I think perhaps I'd better go to Sydney. There's not much I can do here really, and I do want to see Guy.'

'You'd better ask Grenville about it,' said Gilly, heaping shredded lettuce in a wooden bowl.

Lesley took a slice of cucumber and nibbled at it. Why should she ask Grenville? And if Grenville should decide to say no, would she have to meekly accept his decree? She *had* to see Guy ... She said mildly, 'I'll only stay a day or two. Surely Grenville' – the name slipped out unconsciously and she blushed in confusion—' surely Dr. Garrison won't cavil at that.'

Tracy arrived home then, and so no more was said.

After lunch, Lesley went to her room to lie down for a few minutes. It was a hot day, and a warm wind was making the flimsy nylon curtains billow softly into the room. Lesley lay on the bed watching them and trying to relax. What would come out of her next meeting with Guy? Would he want to make marriage plans? Did that other girl – Miss Burke – mean anything in his life? And if she did, did Lesley mind so terribly much? Somehow she didn't. She felt badly unsettled and most unsettling of all was this knowledge that she was by no means ready to rush into marriage with Guy – however badly she needed a husband to be a father to Jane. These two past years had set her and Guy so far apart from each other that all she had felt for him at nineteen seemed to have vanished into nothingness. That didn't say much for what she had taken so unquestioningly to be love.

She tried to call up an image of his face in her mind, but his altered, mature appearance defeated her, and as she finally slipped into mindlessness and sleep, it was Grenville Garrison's image that floated before her – his thick black hair, his eyes, so searching and mystical . . .

She was startled awake by Sister Gilbert's voice calling to her.

'Lesley, Grenville wants you over at the hospital at

once.'

Lesley sat up, her heart beating wildly. She slid off the bed, slipped her feet into sandals, dragged a comb through her tangled hair. Something terrible had happened – and she had not been there—

She hurried along the verandah to where Gilly sat rocking Tracy's baby.

Gilly stared at Lesley, whose eyes were wide and tragic.

'For heaven's sake, child, there's no need to look like that! Your little niece has regained consciousness.'

Lesley stared, laughed and began to run.

In the elevator, she realized what a mess she must look, her hair hanging loose, her cotton dress crumpled. But of course it didn't matter. What did matter was that Jane must be definitely on the mend – and that Grenville Garrison wanted her there. When she reached the small room, he was waiting for her, and Nurse Warren was standing by the cot.

'This is what we've been waiting for, Lesley,' he said, and he smiled at her, took her hand and drew her across the room. Jane's eyes were open. They were a dark and smoky blue – like Linda's and like Lesley's – and they looked enormous in her little white face. Lesley touched her cheek gently and leaned down towards her. The child closed her eyes and turned her face into the pillow with a little sound like a whimper. She looked exhausted. Lesley whispered, 'Jane, I'm here, darling. I'm Aunty Lesley.'

She stayed by the child for the rest of the afternoon.

Jane opened her eyes again several times, and she stared at Lesley for a long time. Once she managed the vestige of a smile. At teatime someone brought Lesley a tray with steamed chicken and peas and potatoes under a cover, and she ate it hungrily, and drank the cup of tea a junior nurse brought her.

When she went back to Leura House, worn out but very much cheered, no one was about except Gilly who was in the kitchen ironing.

'So Jane's on the mend,' she said with an affectionate smile as Lesley came in. 'You must feel as though you've been given a million dollars.'

'I do,' admitted Lesley. 'I felt so depressed, so useless, today. Oh, heavens! I must telephone Guy. I can't possibly go to Sydney now—'

She dashed back into the hall and soon had got through to Guy.

'Okay for tomorrow, honey?' he asked when they had greeted each other.

'Guy – no, it's just not the right time. Jane's so much better, I'll have to stay here so that she can get used to me, get to know me.'

There was silence for a moment. Then, 'That's great about the kid, but I'm disappointed you don't feel you can spare a day or two.'

'I'm sorry. Couldn't you come down on Sunday?'

'Afraid not. As a matter of fact, Lesley, I've accepted an invitation for both of us to join a party going up the Hawkesbury on a motor cruiser. I thought it

58

would give you a kick.'

'I'd have loved it,' said Lesley – though she would have infinitely preferred a quiet weekend with Guy, under the circumstances. 'But just the same, couldn't you—'

'Put it off? Don't ask it of me, honey! It happens to be a convenient way of meeting socially a client whose account I'm angling for. If I get the account, I get my promotion. It's pretty important. In fact if you positively decide you can't be here, I'll just have to take some other girl along. I can't upset the party. It just does make it a little difficult when I've said I'm bringing my fiancée.'

He paused, and Lesley wrestled with a moment's indecision. In a way, she had the choice of helping Guy or helping Jane – and she rather thought Guy was the one who could manage best without her. As for the necessity of taking another girl – she very nearly asked, 'Won't Miss Burke oblige?'

Very nearly but not quite.

Footsteps crossed the verandah from the garden, and she knew instinctively that it was Grenville Garrison. She turned her head slightly and he smiled at her. She thought she had gained a little ground with him lately – and today he had actually called her Lesley. It would not do for him to suspect that all was not as it should be between herself and Guy. She said brightly and deliberately into the mouthpiece, 'I'm terribly sorry about that, Guy darling. But just do whatever you think best. I'll understand . . . Anyhow, next weekend should be safe.'

'Let's hope so,' he said. He sounded slightly offended. 'I'd appreciate it more if you could be here this Sunday. It's not good for the ego having you disappear before I've even been able to show you around to everyone.'

She rang off a moment later, and she didn't go back to the kitchen. *He* was there, and she didn't feel inclined to prevaricate tonight.

She slept exhaustedly that night, and woke at six o'clock in the morning, her thoughts flying eagerly to Jane. She dressed quickly and went to the kitchen to make some breakfast. Tracy was there and beamed as she appeared.

'Terrific developments! I'm so glad. You must be excited.'

'I am,' said Lesley. Everyone seemed interested in Jane and pleased that she was making such progress. Lesley got herself some breakfast and went over to the hospital. Jane had slept well, the nurse told her, and now she was awake and her smoky blue eyes looked at Lesley questioningly. Lesley was allowed to feed her, but she was only pecking, and soon her eyelids closed and she began to cry fretfully. Nurse Warren came to take over.

'She'll be asleep in a sec,' she said. 'You go and have a break, Miss Brooke.'

The Sister spoke to her after she left Jane's room.

'Come back as soon as you like, dear. Dr. Garrison says it's important. They flick their eyes open sometimes, these babies that can't make up their minds whether to stay or to be gone, and if Mummy's there it makes all the difference. I've seen it many times.' Lesley wanted to remind her that she was not Jane's mother, but in the face of those steady honest eyes she couldn't. 'Dr. Garrison was three years in England and America on a research scholarship,' went on Sister, who was in a chatty mood. 'Some people say he's wasted down the coast here, that he should be at one of the big city hospitals. But we need him here – I don't know what we'd do without him.' Her cheery smile flashed out. 'Well, I mustn't stand here talking all day. We'll see you a little later, shall we?'

'Yes, of course,' agreed Lesley.

Jane picked up condition rapidly during the next few days. She seemed to accept Lesley, and her air of exhaustion began to fade. She was eating a little more, but there were times when she rejected everyone and everything and wept fretfully, and no one could help her. Grenville Garrison told Lesley, who stayed in the little room most of the day, 'Keep at it – you're doing a good job there, Miss Brooke. Not had enough of it yet?'

'No.'

'And the fiancè?' He frowned slightly. 'It's a pity he hasn't managed to come down to Balgola. There's no future in letting you win the child's love and trust if she's going to wake up one day and find you gone for good.'

Lesley bit her lip. Why couldn't he believe in her? He had praised her only a moment ago. She wished very much that she could confront him with a fiancé who was not only willing, but positively eager to adopt a two-year-old child. But she would have to be something of a magician to do that . . .

Barbara White was discharged from the hospital that day, and the next morning, with Rory and Deedee gone, Leura House seemed strangely empty – though Gilly assured Lesley that it would be a short-lived peace. Over the breakfast washing up, Lesley asked her curiously, 'Has Dr. Garrison ever married, Gilly?'

The other woman gave her a sharp look. 'I thought the gossips would have brought you up to date on that by now, Lesley.'

'No,' said Lesley. 'I haven't heard a thing. I just don't believe there is such a thing as gossip about Grenville Garrison. No one has anything but praise for him.'

'And you don't think that's right? Just because he was a little hard on you when you first arrived?'

Lesley said, 'He was *very* hard on me. But I suppose he thought he had good reason.'

'Hmm,' said Gilly, and Lesley wondered if in her heart she agreed with the doctor, though she was too kind or too tactful to question Lesley. No doubt her philosophy, often a wise one, was least said, soonest mended. At all events, Lesley was doing the right thing now. 'Well,' she continued after a moment, 'Grenville was married once. In fact, he married almost as soon as he was through medical school. It was a girl from Melbourne, Alison Mortimer.'

'What happened?'

'She was accidentally drowned.'

Lesley was shocked. 'How terrible! Was she very young?'

'Twenty-two, I believe. After it happened, Grenville went overseas on a research fellowship. It was a good thing for him to get right away, but somehow he's never got over it. He never speaks of it at all, not even to me, and I've known him practically all his life. He's buried himself in his work – much to the annoyance of all the young women around the district who find him attractive.' She sighed. 'Ah well, there's nothing much we can do about it, is there?'

Lesley agreed that there was nothing. She thought that in a way he was an impossibly remote and hard man, and yet she had glimpsed an occasional gleam of tenderness somewhere. And she had to admit that the children in the hospital all seemed to love him. As did their mothers!

She was, rather to her surprise, generally accepted into the circle of mothers without question, just as if she were one of themselves. Many times she heard a friendly inquiry as to how Jane was getting on, and she had received several offers of toys or books of nursery rhymes and so on – 'for when that poor little pet of a child is looking for something to amuse her'.

However, they were not all pleasant and friendly. There was one exception, Mrs. Nelson, an attractive,

63

well-dressed woman whose dark hair always looked as if she had come straight from the hairdressers. She didn't stay at Leura House, she was a local woman, and very happily married to the jeweller whose shop Lesley had seen sometimes when she went down to the town. On two occasions at least when Grenville Garrison had stopped to speak to Lesley about Jane, this woman had interrupted with a request.

'Dr. Garrison, Marie-Anna has developed a little cough. Sister says it's nothing, but I'd like *you* to listen to her chest while you're here—' And on this particular day it was, 'Doctor, Marie-Anna has this rash. Could it be measles?'

Lesley saw his eyebrows go up, but he smiled pleasantly, excused himself to Lesley, and went. Lesley wondered, 'Is she a man-eater? Or is she just an over-conscientious mother?' She felt a little sorry for Marie-Anne who she suspected must be more fussed over than was good for her.

As she was leaving the hospital that day she found herself in Mrs. Nelson's company. She smiled, but the dark-haired woman gave her a look that could hardly be called friendly, and was even verging upon venomous. Lesley asked pleasantly, 'How is Marie-Anna, Mrs. Nelson? I hope she doesn't have the measles.'

'She has a very nasty heat rash.'

'Poor child! Does she have to stay long in hospital?'

The other woman shrugged. 'She suffers badly with bronchitis. I simply can't manage her at home – we're

64

both of us so highly strung. I suppose you're hoping it will be a long while yet before your niece is able to leave. Lovely for you!'

Lesley looked at her, puzzled. 'Lovely for me?'

The other woman gave a cynical laugh. 'Well, it's no secret that you enjoy your important little *tête-à-têtes* with the handsome doctor. However, I should warn you that you'll find him quite impervious to feminine charms. I've known Grenville for several years, and he won't look at another woman since he lost his wife. If I were you, I should save my efforts for someone more susceptible in the absence of your fiancé.'

Lesley's cheeks reddened angrily, but she said nothing. She was not going to be provoked into a senseless slanging match.

'It's your niece he's interested in, if you're in any doubt,' Mrs. Nelson continued persistently, quickening her pace to keep up with Lesley as they went down the long drive. 'He'll go out of his way to immense lengths to look after any child who's had as bad a time as poor little Jane Jarmyn.'

Lesley said evenly, 'She did have a bad time. However, she's getting over it now.'

'It's a wonder she's still alive, in my view,' said the other woman cruelly. 'It's certainly no thanks to her parents, and I say it even if her mother was your sister. They'd both been drinking, and he must have been driving like a maniac in all that rain. Then to leave the child to sink with the car! The boot was loaded up with liquor – I heard it from friends who were at the Whistling Duck Motel in Merrigal the same night. Just loaded! It was there when the car was dragged out of the river.'

Lesley was shaking. Her face was dead white, and she could scarcely believe this woman was saying the things she heard. She stood stock still and looked at Mrs. Nelson steadily. 'You have no right to say any of those – malicious things. You can't possibly know what happened. And my sister would never have drunk too much – would never have left a child to drown – never—'

'My dear girl, it was all in the newspapers. You must have read the reports. Wasn't it shame that kept you from coming here earlier? It's not my fault the Jarmyns were as they were – loose-living, immoral artist types, out for kicks. Living beyond their income – leaving debts behind them wherever they went. Why, they didn't even stay their night out at the motel, they got the wind up about something or other. I think it was—'

At that point Lesley, who was burning with a sort of helpless anger, interrupted sharply. 'I don't want to hear what you think, Mrs. Nelson. And please, just never – never – speak to me again! You're a – a wicked woman, to talk like that—'

Tears stung her eyes as she walked quickly away. Her feet carried her through the hospital gates, along the road, through the scented garden to Leura House. She saw nothing, her mind was in a turmoil, and she could not rid herself of the things that hateful vindictive woman had said. Things that could not possibly be true – not possibly. Linda was not a loose-living, immoral type. Linda would have thought of her child before ever she thought of herself. And yet – they *could* have been living beyond their income. Grenville Garrison had said that Tony had left nothing.

There was just that one small grain of truth.

Badly disturbed, Lesley thought, 'It's so long since I really knew Linda.' Could she have changed? In some ways of course she was bound to have done so – but not as drastically as that. Not possibly.

When she went into the house there was a letter for her from Guy, that had come in the afternoon mail. She opened it abstractedly, her eyes skimming over the one short page without much interest. 'You'll be glad to know it looks like I might have landed that account,' she read, 'though it might take another social weekend to clinch it.' He was sorry she had missed the 'beaut day on the river', and he hoped all was going well in her neck of the woods. Emma, by the way, was back from her holiday and said that Lesley was welcome to share her flat any time she came to Sydney. 'Love, Guy.'

None of it seemed to mean much to her. Of course she was pleased that Guy was doing well, but it all seemed unreal, part of a world in which she did not live and never would. And she wondered vaguely about Emma.

That night she got through dinner hardly aware of what was going on around her, and afterwards, instead of helping Gilly with the washing up as she usually did, she murmured something about taking a walk by the sea and set out for the small secluded beach on the south side of the headland.

It was a beautiful night, the dark sky brilliant with stars, the sea a mysterious godlike creature that rode in magnificently over the crescent of silver sand, shouting its triumph, then, hushing and murmuring, retreated to ride in again. Lesley discarded her sandals near the foot of the cliffside track and walked slowly along at the edge of the water, letting it swirl about her feet. She tried to think only of the beauty and peace about her, of the delights of her senses. Not to be cerebral and tense. To let the darkness and the night air and the sounds of the sea exorcize the ugliness and cruelty of that woman's vicious gossip about the Jarmyns. But she could not control the direction her mind was determined to take. It had rankled to have Mrs. Nelson insinuate she was throwing herself at Grenville Garrison, trying to monopolize and even to intrigue him. Nothing could have been further from Lesley's thoughts. He was the last man she would ever attempt to intrigue. She was ready to admit he had done a great deal for Jane, and that he truly had the child's welfare at heart. Unfortunately his distrust of her own sincerity had been based on a reason valid to him, and one that she was in no position to demonstrate was not actually valid at all.

She gasped suddenly as a wave larger than the rest broke only two feet away from her and the water swirled madly around her legs, drenching most of her cotton dress and scattering spray over her face and hair.

So much for concentrating on the pleasures of the

night, and soothing her troubled mind! Intent on thoughts she had been determined not to have, she had walked further into the sea than she had realized, and now, her sopping dress clinging to her slender form, she turned back to the shore and hurried on to the firm sand out of the water's reach.

Someone else was on the beach now. A tall shadow came towards her purposefully, and Lesley knew a brief moment of fear. Then a familiar voice said, 'Hello, Lesley Brooke,' and she realized it was Bob Prescott. 'The stars said I'd be lucky tonight, and so I am. I've been haunting this beach at night like the ghost of a shipwrecked sailor, and never till now caught so much as a sight of you. I'd begun to wonder if you'd gone. How are things?'

'They're fine,' said Lesley, though it was not quite the truth.

'That's great. I thought for a minute just now that you'd decided to do away with yourself, walking into the sea like that.'

'It was unintentional.' Lesley pushed back her tumbled hair with a hand that was sticky with salt spray. 'I wasn't thinking where I was going. My dress is soaked,' she added ruefully. 'I'll have to go home and get out of it.'

'Oh, don't go yet,' he protested. 'It's a warm night — you won't catch pneumonia. A walk to the end of the beach and back and you'll be dry and respectable.' He took her arm persuasively. 'And while we walk you can tell me what's on your mind that's made you so forgetful of your surroundings. I take it the little Jarmyn kid's still well and truly in the land of the living.'

'Yes, she's progressing marvellously.' Lesley took a few reluctant steps along the beach. She had no intention of walking as far as he had suggested, and she was certainly not going to confide in him. In a minute she would insist on going back to Leura House – she was uncomfortably wet, and moreover, remembering that wicked look in Bob Prescott's eyes, she was far from sure of the advisability of walking in the darkness of the night with him.

'And how's the fiancé? I don't wish him any harm, but—'

'Guy will be down here again next weekend,' said Lesley firmly, though that she did not believe, from the tone of his letter. Still, it was preferable that Bob should believe it. His arm had been withdrawn from hers and was now warmly and possessively around her waist, regardless of her wetness. She added, 'And now, please, I must go back to Leura House and get out of these wet clothes.'

He groaned. 'Marching orders! Why do you have to be such a happily engaged girl, Lesley? You're just the type I could really fall for – slim and blonde and fair-skinned, with a pretty voice and none of the hideous eccentricities that most of my fellow-students affect these days. Still, it's a bit of a shame you so obviously don't believe in Women's Lib.'

Lesley didn't answer. He had stopped in his tracks and was holding her firmly by both arms and looking down into her face with the very obvious intention of kissing her. Lesley most definitely didn't want to be kissed by Bob Prescott, but she didn't see that she had a chance of escaping from those strong hands of his. Then, at the crucial moment, just before his lips reached hers, she asked in a dauntingly matter-of-fact voice — although her heart was thudding nervously, 'Bob, did you ever meet my sister or Tony Jarmyn?'

Her tactics actually worked. He raised his head and said with a grimace, 'I get it. No kisses. Nothing. All right, Lesley girl ... No, I never met the Jarmyns. If you really want to talk about them — if that caper isn't simply a ruse to get rid of my attentions — then you'll have to call at the pub and see my old man. If you make it at night, you might run into me. If you come during the day you might escape me — I work in the bar then.'

Lesley gave him a slightly ashamed look. 'I'm sorry about that. I probably will come during the day, though, but mostly because I don't go out at night much ... And now I think I'll find my sandals and go home.' She twisted adroitly from his arms before he could tighten his hold, and resignedly he accompanied her across the sand.

They climbed the narrow winding track together and parted, to Lesley's relief, when they reached the road. She paused near a street lamp to survey herself with dismay, and push back her damp tangled hair.

When she looked up again it was straight into the disapproving face of Grenville Garrison.

CHAPTER FOUR

IN the light of the street lamp his eyes made a thorough appraisal of her – the clinging lines of her wet dress, the disarray of her hair, her wide eyes.

'What on earth are you about, Miss Brooke?' he demanded harshly. 'Because you're having problems with your fiancé do you have to seek consolation in that particular way?'

'In – in what particular way?' Lesley asked, her breath uneven. Had he seen her on the beach with Bob? Did he imagine he had been witnessing some sort of a love scene? He had and he did, she soon discovered.

'Playing about in the sea – offering your kisses on the beach to someone who's obviously in search of nothing more than a little light sexual entertainment.'

Lesley gasped. So that was what he thought of her! She was stung to instant anger.

'You certainly jump to conclusions, don't you, Dr. Garrison? You're determined to think the worst of me. Did you by any chance come here especially to check up on my movements? And who told you where I was?' At the back of her mind was the dismaying thought that any advance she had lately made in his estimation was now wiped out completely. She was right back to where she had been that very first day – and that was way, way down.

He said aloofly, 'Sister Gilbert told me you were depressed, that you'd gone to take a walk by the sea. And I came after you not for the reason you appear to suspect but to talk over with you the cause of your depression – which I presume to be connected with your fiancé's latest letter and his probable unwillingness to share the burden of your niece.'

Lesley thought about that for a moment. It certainly sounded reasonable enough, but he was completely wrong about the cause of her depression. However, she was not going to tell him of Mrs. Nelson's allegations about her sister – or of her insinuations about herself and Grenville. Nor, of course, did she intend to discuss Guy with him.

'And now,' she challenged, 'now that you've – caught me out, as you think – now I suppose there's no need for discussion. Now you'll put another cross against my name – deduct another point, make a derogatory note in my dossier, my file. "Miss Brooke is not fit to be placed in charge of an innocent child. She is – she is promiscuous".'

She shivered a little in her wet clothing, despite the warmth of the night, and she thought she saw a grim smile flit across his face. Whether it was her plight that amused him or something she had said she did not know, and when he spoke he sounded exasperated.

'Why do you take this attitude – say these impossible, irrational – *childish* things?'

'Are they irrational? When I've been misjudged?

73

When all I've done is—' She broke off and flung out her hands in a futile gesture. 'You don't *want* me to have Jane, do you?'

'No, I don't think I do,' he said after a second. 'Because Jane deserves two parents – two willing, loving parents.' He took her roughly by the arm. 'You're shivering, you foolish girl. Come along and we'll get you home.'

Lesley hurried along at his side, her teeth chattering, though she knew it was more from a kind of nervousness than from anything else.

'Jane doesn't have even one parent,' she said. 'Any child can start off with two and then have one – or none.'

'Sadly enough that's true. But at least we can see that Jane starts afresh in the usual way.'

'What makes you think she won't do that with me and – and Guy? When we're married—' Her voice faltered. She glanced up at him and saw his dark brows tilt sardonically.

'Exactly. And that brings us back again to the little matter of your depression. *When* – the operative word. For your marriage won't happen till you see things Guy Longden's way.'

'Why not?' retorted Lesley. They had reached the Leura House gate and stepped inside, but they stood there staring at each other with hostility.

'A pretty face and figure may count for a great deal, but they won't get you your own way in everything,' he said laconically. 'Few men want to start their lives lumbered with someone else's children.'

'How would you know whether Guy felt that way or not?' she flashed.

'How would you think, Lesley?'

Lesley. Her mind registered the disturbing use of her first name despite her angry agitation.

'You've rung him – you've talked to him,' she floundered. 'Oh, how despicable, to go behind my back like that! To – why did you do it?' she breathed, appalled.

'You are the one who is jumping to conclusions now,' he said coolly. 'I didn't ring Guy. Your own attitude – your constant evasions – have told me the truth. Do you think I'm a fool to be so easily duped? Then tonight you get a letter, you're depressed, you go out seeking some kind of consolation ... Add to that the fact that your fiancé has never come here since that first day – it hardly indicates enthusiasm. And don't tell me it's business that's kept him away. If his heart were in it, he'd be here.'

Lesley groped for words. Her wild accusation was wrong, but it could so easily have been right. 'It *has* been business – I understand that, even if you don't. And if you leave me alone, I will persuade Guy. Besides, none of it's your concern – I am Jane's *aunt*—'

'And I am her doctor,' he said. 'Any child under my care is to some extent my concern. Would you think better of me if I didn't care what happened to Jane?'

'Doctors and nurses can't afford to care,' she flung at

him. 'They have their work to do, but – but they'd destroy themselves if they allowed themselves to become too personally involved.'

In the starlight those eyes, those dark, see-everything eyes that had something mystical in their depth travelled slowly over her face, flicked down her slender form in the bedraggled dress, came back to her mussed-up ashy hair and then to her mouth, full-lipped, soft, rebellious.

'You know,' he said enigmatically, a strange note in his voice, 'you're more than half-way right, Lesley . . . Now run along inside and get changed. We'll talk about it some other time . . . Good night.' He opened the gate, stepped through and closed it behind him and was gone.

Lesley stood for a minute, her lower lip caught between her small white teeth. She was annoyed with herself for attacking him as she had. That would get her nowhere. Had she been spoiling for a fight in reaction against the mental upset Mrs. Nelson had caused her? Wouldn't it have been wiser by far to have remained cool and calm, to have explained rationally what had happened on the beach, and why her dress was soaked? But he had provoked her by his assumption that she had been engaged in some kind of a – a sexual frolic with Bob Prescott, when she had not even allowed Bob to kiss her! It was annoying to say the least of it. She knew somehow that it had not been because of Guy that she had shrunk from that kiss. It had been because of something deep within herself that she had not yet examined, and could not now put her finger on. It was like quicksilver – when she tried to capture it, it eluded her.

And now, she thought, walking slowly towards the house, she had left herself open to further disapproval. She would have to do much better than that in future or she could not possibly hope to win her battle against Grenville Garrison's prejudices.

The following day there were new patients in the children's ward, more mothers with young children at Leura House. Sister told Lesley that Jane was no longer to be isolated, she was to be moved into the ward. Lesley was suddenly so busy she no longer had time to worry or to fret over recent events. Jane knew her now and she began to feel rewarded as well as useful. If she had vague fears that Grenville would cancel out her previous privileges, then they were unfounded. She continued to be treated as if Jane were her own child.

The weekend came. Guy confirmed that he couldn't make it, but this time she was not pressed – or even invited – to join the party, wherever it was to be. Lesley began to think that he must be just as occupied with his work during weekends as he was during the week. She wondered which girl he had taken along to the Hawkesbury and if he was taking the same partner to this weekend's party. Maybe it was the obliging Miss Burke! But as she had more or less declined to be at his side, she was hardly in a position to inquire. That was odd, she reflected. She didn't know the man she was engaged to well enough to ask him a simple question without fearing he might think she was prying.

That Saturday Grenville, of whom, since the night of the beach fracas, she had seen very little, spoke to her in the ward.

'I'd like a word with you in the downstairs office, Miss Brooke. In twenty minutes' time.'

Lesley immediately flew into a panic. He was going to tell her she must go – the hospital doors would be closed to her, there would be no room for her at Leura House. She was suddenly all too well aware of the power that Grenville Garrison wielded. He could certainly have her out of here in a flash if he decided to do so. And what, after all, did she have to offer Jane in the way of a future? Was she not being foolish – even selfish – in hanging on as she did? And just why did she do it? Lesley couldn't have answered that question herself. Reason told her that she should hand Jane over to other loving hearts. Her own heart told her that she was here now to love and comfort her and that the time to go would be when she knew there was someone else right there to take her place. Surely a little loving now could do no harm. And yet it all went deeper than that. She stayed because some inner voice told her to stay – even against all reason.

But if Grenville decreed that she should go, if he set the wheels in motion, then she was finished.

She went down to the small office with fear in her heart, her face pale, her eyes wide.

The interview was not as she had imagined it.

Nothing was said about their last encounter, so perhaps on that score, he had decided to forgive and to forget. And though Lesley would have welcomed an opportunity of vindicating herself as far as his mis-interpretation of what had happened on the beach went, she did not have one.

He stood, smiled pleasantly, and asked her to be seated. There were red roses in the room again, and they drew Lesley's eyes constantly, and she found their scent more unnerving than before.

'Jane is improving at such a rate now, Miss Brooke, that we must both give some very serious thought to her future. I'm sure you are sensible enough to agree that if your fiancé is not interested in taking her, then it will be best for you to give her up.' He glanced across the desk at her, his dark grey eyes steady and searching. 'I'm not trying to bully you, or to frighten you, I'm simply trying to give you some practical and helpful advice. You have a very charming way with children and they like you – I'm referring not only to Jane but to numer-ous other children to whom you've given some of your time. To Rory, to little Sally Tressider, to the Nelson child—'

Lesley moved uneasily and shifted her gaze to the flowers. She didn't know he had been aware of the time she had spent with other children, and she hoped he didn't know that she had been requested to leave Marie-Anna Nelson alone – by her mother.

'However,' he continued, and he too glanced at the

79

roses and frowned slightly, 'even if you are deprived of Jane, you will no doubt have children of your own one day. Please keep that in mind when I tell you quite simply that there are plenty of good women already married and unable to have children of their own who would give Jane a true mother's love.'

Lesley's lashes flew up and her mouth opened in protest, but he raised·a silencing hand.

'Let me finish, please. You're a nice girl, Miss Brooke.' He smiled slightly as he said this and Lesley coloured and wondered, 'Is that meant sarcastically? Is he thinking of my sins? – of the long, long time it took me to come to my niece, of the naughty scene he witnessed the other night?'

'And you're entitled to happiness,' he said. 'I'm not going to let you wreck your chances of a happy marriage quite unnecessarily on these particular rocks. Whoever takes the child will love her quite as much as you do, will cherish her as you would want her to be cherished, and in fact, I have a particular young woman in mind, Judy Barnett – you'd like her, I promise you. But before we take any radical steps, I think you should have your chance. You told me the other night that if I left you alone, you could persuade Guy Longden to think as you do. So I suggest you arrange to go to Sydney to do exactly that. Does that seem fair – reasonable?'

Lesley bit her lip. It seemed very fair. It was, of course, forcing the issue, and she knew what Grenville Garrison did not – that there were far more things to be discussed by Guy Longden and Lesley Brooke before they set the date of their marriage than whether or not they would adopt Jane.

'You don't want to go to Sydney?' he pressed when she was silent.

'Yes – yes, of course I do. But Guy is working and—'

'You should have gone this weekend. However, I'm sure you'll find plenty to amuse you while your fiancé is at work. Most women enjoy shopping, and you must have friends you want to see again.'

Lesley shook her head. 'I don't have money to spend shopping. And I don't have any friends in Sydney.'

'No friends?' His glance sharpened. 'How long have you been in Australia, Miss Brooke? Long enough to meet Guy Longden and fall in love with him?'

Lesley wished that she could control the colour that had crept into her face. 'I knew Guy before I came to Australia,' she said evasively, and hurried on, 'But I should like to look up the people in the flats where my sister used to live.'

'Why?' he shot out.

'Why, to – to talk to them about Linda,' she said in surprise, though she knew her motive went deeper than that. 'It's some time since we saw one another, and I—'

He frowned. 'I shouldn't waste time doing that,' he told her, a guarded look on his face. 'There's no point in it – none at all.'

No point in it? What did that mean? Lesley wondered. Mrs. Nelson had said, Most people share my opinion of the Jarmyns. Did Grenville Garrison too think Lesley's sister had been a loose-living, immoral type who— She checked her thoughts abruptly. If he thought that, did he think the same might apply to her, Lesley? Was that why he was keeping such a close watch on her, and was so ready to expect the worst of her? She would certainly have to watch her step. Perhaps she was imagining all this, and yet – he had asked her how well she had known her sister. And now he was warning her not to look up the people who had known the Jarmyns.

She knew a pang of fear and uncertainty. But it could not be true.

She said calmly, 'To me there is a point, Dr. Garrison.' She pushed back her pale blonde hair. 'Was that all you had to say to me?'

'I think so, yes.' He rose and saw her to the door, and before she went out he said, 'Remember what I've said, won't you, Lesley. Arrange your trip to Sydney. And keep in mind that I have the best possible motives in advising you.'

She nodded and hurried away. That casual, easy, almost intimate use of her name – that sudden adoption of a personal note – had done extraordinary things to her, had turned her limbs momentarily to water. And she could not imagine why. She occupied herself in wondering whether his final words had been an underlining of his advice about Jane in general, or his advice not to look up Linda's old friends . . .

Of course, thought Lesley when she awoke the next morning after a troubled night, there was someone else available who had known the Jarmyns. She had only to go into town and talk to Bob Prescott's father at the Pacific Hotel and she would learn something about Linda and Tony. She would learn for sure that Mrs. Nelson was nothing but a spiteful gossip . . . She decided to put it to the test that very day. Jane usually slept after lunch, so early in the afternoon she told Sister Gilbert that she was going out for a while. She caught the bus that ran between hospital and town to fit in with visiting hours, left it at the corner of Ocean Road, and in a matter of minutes was at the Pacific Hotel. In the lounge she asked a friendly middle-aged woman where she could find Mr. Prescott.

'Go through to the inside terrace, dear,' she was told. 'Across the courtyard you'll find a door marked Private. Knock on that and you'll have him.'

Lesley did as she was told, and waited nervously for someone to come to the door. She assured herself that soon she would hear the truth about Linda, and she would be satisfied.

The man who opened the door was middle-aged, over-weight and pleasant. He had evidently been resting. His shirt sleeves were rolled up and he wore no tie, and no shoes. He asked her ruefully, 'What is it?'

'I've disturbed you,' Lesley apologized. 'I'm sorry. I'm Leslie Brooke, and I wanted to – to talk to you about my sister and brother-in-law, Linda and Tony Jarmyn.'

83

He frowned a little. 'I see. Come in, won't you?'

She stepped into a pleasant living-room where a television set was still on, and where a large table, one end of which was littered with papers and books, occupied a good part of the space. Mr. Prescott switched off the television and gestured to her to take a chair. When she was seated he returned to the couch where he had evidently had his feet up when she had knocked.

'How is the little girl?'

Lesley managed a smile. 'Coming along, thank you.'

'I'm glad of that. Sad for her being left on her own.'

'Yes. Did you know my sister well?'

'I wouldn't say well.' He reached for cigarettes and offered her one, and when she refused lit a cigar for himself, taking his time over it. 'No, I couldn't say I knew her well. Tony stayed here often, now and again she came along too. She was quite a girl! I guess they liked to get away together to have a bit of a break. To tell the truth, I never knew they had a kiddie till the accident happened.' He looked across at her through narrowed eyes. 'You're nothing like your sister, are you? Both blondes – though you're much fairer – but that's about all. Lot of age difference, and you're' – he smiled a little – 'the more ladylike.'

Lesley bit her lip. 'People used to say we were alike. Our eyes,' she suggested.

He looked at her intently. 'I don't notice eyes all that much ... It was a terrible tragedy, wasn't it? Shocking! Still, I reckon they had their money's worth of good times. Lived hard and squeezed out the last possible drop of enjoyment from it all. It's something.'

Lesley looked at him uncomprehendingly. That didn't sound like Linda's sort of life.

'Yes,' he said musingly. 'They did everything with all their might, and they were great company. Drinking, laughing, loving, telling funny stories – well, you name it.'

Suddenly Lesley didn't want to hear any more. She had come here to be comforted and reassured and she had been neither. She stood up feeling slightly sick. She said faintly, 'Thank you, Mr. Prescott,' and moved across the room towards the door.

He got up too and sent her a quizzical look. His fingers round the door handle, he said, 'If you're worried they may have owed me money, Miss Brooke – they didn't. Not a cent. As far as I'm concerned Tony Jarmyn was a good bloke. He took what he wanted from life, and to my mind he only cheated you if you asked for it.' He gave her a sudden paternal smile. 'Was that what you wanted to know?'

'Not – really,' said Lesley. 'But thank you all the same.'

'You're welcome.'

She escaped into the heat of the street. Opposite, the Pacific Ocean rolled in endlessly, blue-green and beautiful under a blue sky where a few flimsy white clouds drifted low against the horizon. Lesley didn't wait for the bus. She walked slowly along the water-

85

front, and up the long slow hill towards the hospital and Leura House, and she thought of Mr. Prescott's testimony. He had liked Tony and Linda. That much was clear. He was not spiteful and cruel like Mrs. Nelson. And yet Lesley was no happier now than she had been earlier. She hadn't heard what she wanted to hear, by any means.

By the time she reached Leura House, she had made a decision. She went straight through to the kitchen. Gilly was making tomato pickle and there was a smell of spices and vinegar in the air. She paused to sniff it and to say appreciatively, 'Smells great!' and then – unobtrusively, she hoped – she slipped through to the laundry. She knew there was a pile of old newspapers there and she had made up her mind she would look for a report of the accident.

It took her a long while to find anything. The papers were jumbled, and she was not certain of the date. But eventually she found two accounts, and sitting in a wooden chair she read them.

'In the early hours of this morning in heavy rain, a car went over the bank of the flooded river beyond Merrigal on the far south coast. The occupants of the car, Tony Jarmyn, commercial artist, aged thirty-three, and his wife, a beautiful blonde, managed to free themselves by forcing open the door before the car sank, but neither of them was able to reach the shore. Their baby daughter was washed through the open back window. She was seen by Mr. Dick Leeming, a truck-driver, who had pulled up for a rest. "I thought it was

86

just a bit of flotsam drifting down," he told reporters later. When the "flotsam" was caught in the branches of a fallen tree, he went to investigate and found the child. He performed mouth-to-mouth resuscitation on the bank before taking her to the hospital at Balgola Bay, where her condition is serious. The bodies of Mr. and Mrs. Jarmyn were recovered at midday, a mile and a half downstream. It is believed the couple were motoring to Melbourne.'

There was something chilling and terribly unreal about the acccount. Lesley could not get it into her head that she was reading about Linda. Those words, 'his wife, a beautiful blonde', sounded so utterly false. Pretty warm-hearted Linda, with her light brown hair, reduced to a meaningless phrase to titillate the minds of a sensation-loving public.

The second account was far more sensational and over-dramatized, and she read it reluctantly and with a feeling of repugnance. There was a clear insinuation that the baby had been abandoned, and that the reason for the parents not reaching safety had been a 'celebration party' held earlier at a motel, which they had left in something of a hurry. Under cover of maudlin detail – 'picture these two light-hearted people only an hour or so earlier, holiday bent, and sure that what lay ahead of them was a lifetime of fun' – it was suggested that they were, as Mrs. Nelson had said, out for kicks.

Lesley let the paper fall from her hands and wished futilely that she had left well alone. She thought rebelliously that none of it was true – none of it. They had no right to libel Linda like that. She was staring ahead of her, her eyes swimming with tears, when the half closed door was pushed open and Grenville Garrison came in.

'What the devil are you doing out here, Lesley?'

'I'm reading a lot of lies,' said Lesley, trying to blink away her tears. A spot of colour appeared in each of her otherwise dead white cheeks. 'Lies about my sister.'

He looked at her closely, his hands on his narrow hips.

'Then you're a silly girl. There's no need to disturb yourself.'

'Isn't there? I was disturbed enough already. Someone told me – without mincing matters – exactly what they thought of my sister and her husband. There've been other innuendoes – I realize that now. Even from you. I wanted to find out if it was merely spite or if there was more to it than that.'

'And you looked for your answer in a newspaper?'

Lesley shrugged helplessly. 'I have to look where I can. But this – it just doesn't make sense.' She touched the newspaper contemptuously with the toe of her sandal. 'This is not about my sister. It's – it's cheap sensationalism.'

'Then regard it as such and forget about it.'

'Forget it!' she echoed. 'How can I? Linda would have done everything in her power to save Jane. *Any* mother would have. Even you must allow that.'

'Even I? . . . Yes, I'll allow it. But escaping from a sinking car is a very tricky business. Nobody can tell what really happened. Your brother-in-law obviously knew the importance of getting the doors open before the pressure of water became too great. Your sister might simply have panicked, have lost her wits. It happens. We're all human, we all have human weaknesses and are often at the mercy of uncontrollable physical reactions.' He stopped, taking in Lesley's stricken look, her obvious refusal to accept panic as an excuse. 'Look, Lesley,' he said, his voice harsh, impatient, 'what's happened is over. Nothing can change it. Don't probe. Don't let this sort of rubbish' – and he too touched the newspaper with his foot – 'throw you off balance. Hang on to your memories of your sister as you knew her, and get on with the job in hand.'

'The job in hand!' she echoed incredulously. 'When you're doing your best to see I don't get Jane?' She looked at him with open hostility. Just now it seemed all the world was against her – first this business about Jane, and now it seemed that even Grenville Garrison concurred in all those lies about Linda. 'Please don't pretend you're interested in my personal happiness, Dr. Garrison, for I know very well you're not.'

'Then you're a little idiot.' He seized her suddenly by the shoulders so violently that she was nearly jerked off her feet. She staggered, steadied herself, and her eyes blazed back into his. What she saw in their depths shocked her even more rudely than his touch – and expression so suddenly and so darkly passionate it shook her to the very marrow of her bones. Combined with the burning of his grip upon her arms, the effect was almost stultifyingly electrical.

Her breath caught in her throat and the world stopped turning for a mad dizzying second that seemed to last for ever. And then, physically unkissed but figuratively and surely ravished, she was released.

'You'd better ring your fiancé tonight, Miss Brooke,' he said harshly, 'and arrange that trip to Sydney. Guy Longden will help you come to terms with yourself, I'm sure.'

CHAPTER FIVE

LESLEY didn't ring Guy that night, but strangely enough, he telephoned her the following morning just as she was finishing her breakfast.

'Happy birthday, Lesley!'

She felt a shock of pure surprise. She was twenty-one today and she had completely forgotten it.

'How nice of you to remember, Guy. I had no idea what date it was – I'm just not used to celebrating my birthday in summer, I suppose.'

'That could have something to do with it,' he agreed. 'Not much of a birthday for you, though, all by yourself down there. Do you think you can make it to Sydney over the weekend for a celebration?'

'That would be terrific,' said Lesley a little stiffly. She couldn't help wondering if he would really be able to manage time off to celebrate her birthday – or if it would have to be a function somehow combined with business. 'I'll see what I can do.'

'Great! We can have more fun here than we'd manage all on our own at Balgola Bay.'

'I suppose so,' agreed Lesley. Her mind registered that Jane didn't come into his calculations at all. But after all, why should she? Jane was nothing to him ... 'Shall I be able to stay at Emma's flat?'

'Sure. Any time at all ... Keep in touch, then,

Lesley, and I'll get plans under way. Afraid I have to dash for the ferry now – see you soon, honey, and have a nice day.'

Lesley came away from the telephone feeling deeply unsettled. In one way, Dr. Garrison was right. The sooner she got to Sydney and sorted out her affairs the better – though they were not the affairs he imagined. And then she would maybe have to say good-bye to her plans for adopting Jane, start all over rethinking her life. She didn't know what she would do if she called off her engagement to Guy. As she had told Grenville, she had not finished her training to be a nursery school-teacher. In fact, she had scarcely begun it when she had had to give it up to look after her grandmother.

Things were quiet at Leura House that morning. It was one of those brief respites that happened now and again when there were no small children resident, only mothers. Tomorrow it might be busy again ... Gilly was alone this morning, sitting at the kitchen table over a final cup of tea, and she looked up at Leslie with a smile.

'Time for another cup before you're off and away? There's plenty in the pot.' Lesley nodded and sat down and watched her pour the tea. 'So it's your birthday, Lesley. I couldn't help hearing. How old are you?'

'Twenty-one.'

'Twenty-one! Dear me, that's rather a special age to be! What can we do about it? All I can think of is cooking something specially nice for your dinner. What's your favourite dish?'

'Whatever you cook best,' said Lesley with a smile. 'You're a dear, Gilly, but don't make too much fuss of me.' She dropped a kiss on the older woman's cheek as she left the kitchen, and her heart felt warmed.

She was considerably surprised to receive birthday greetings from Grenville Garrison that afternoon, while she was sitting with Jane in the children's ward. She had bought the child a soft cuddly doll one day when she had gone down to the town, and Jane was beginning to grow very attached to it. She was a tiny scrap of a child, and she still had an exhausted pinched look about her little face. She no longer needed a head bandage, and though her dark hair was beginning to grow again where it had been cut away, it was ragged and hardly beautiful. She was certainly no chubby and cherubic toddler, but Lesley found her sweet and appealing, and her rare smiles were touching. Looking at her now, as she hugged the doll against her fragile body, she realized anew what a tremendous responsibility it would be to take charge of her life. Her heart ached with her own inadequacy. She was startled when Dr. Garrison spoke to her.

'Happy birthday, Miss Brooke. Sister Gilbert tells me you're twenty-one today.'

'Yes – thank you,' said Lesley, looking up at him. His face looked very dark against his white coat and he was smiling at her. Lesley found she couldn't look away. She was trying to read what lay in the depths of his dark watchful eyes. His glance went briefly to Jane, then back to her.

'I shall see you later,' he said, and moved quietly away.

Lesley's heart began to thud sickeningly. Did that mean another confrontation? At least she could tell him that she would be seeing Guy this weekend. Yet why not simply give in, tell him that she was leaving Balgola Bay and that she would like him to arrange for Jane's adoption? It was going to happen eventually — she didn't know why she kept fighting against it.

She looked back at her small niece whose blue eyes reminded her so much of Linda, and tenderness stirred deep within her. 'I'll think it out later,' she decided. Somehow, with the child there before her eyes, she could not bear the idea of parting from her. 'I should never have started it all,' thought Lesley. 'I should have taken more notice of what Grenville told me on that first day, instead of digging my toes in to spite him.'

When she went back to Leura House that evening, Gilly came into the hallway fastening a white opal brooch at the neck of her navy silk dress. Her grey-brown hair was uncovered and looked soft and pretty, and she had dabbed a little powder on her small slightly tip-tilted nose.

'Take a shower and put on your best bib and tucker,' she told Lesley. 'Don't forget it's your birthday.'

Lesley smiled at her affectionately. 'I hope you haven't gone to too much bother, Gilly. You should be able to relax a little while things are slack.'

Gilly's blue eyes twinkled. 'Don't encourage me in

that! It's only being busy that keeps me out of mischief. You ask Gren if that isn't so. I didn't take on this job for love of him, you know – I took it for purely selfish reasons. I'm one of those bossy women who like to throw their weight around.' And, as Lesley began laughingly to protest, she added, 'At any rate, I haven't worn my fingers to the bone cooking a meal. As a matter of fact I've been in the town shopping all afternoon and had afternoon tea with Jean Tressider. You might remind me to tell Gren that they've another lame dog at the rectory to look after – a girl who's in some sort of trouble and has tugged at Ian's heartstrings. It's certainly as well he has an obliging ex-nurse for a sister! ... You trot along now, and get yourself dressed up, Lesley. Orders are no cooking, we dine out tonight.'

Orders? wondered Lesley as she headed for her bedroom along the verandah. As far as she knew, there was only one person who gave Sister Gilbert orders, and that was Grenville Garrison. She wondered a little uneasily if he was paying for them to eat out, and wished a little that her birthday had not been discovered. However, it had been, and she did not intend to appear ungrateful. Gilly was dressed up, and she would dress up too.

After she had showered, she put on a dress of wild silk of a mist blue colour that she had never worn. It was a very romantic dress and she had bought it with Guy in mind, ironically enough. Her blonde hair looked more silvery than ever against its shimmering colour, and she brushed it till it shone, then dabbed scent on her wrists and at the base of her throat. She emerged from her bedroom feeling refreshed and even elegant, and went round to the front verandah. Soft light shone from the sitting room windows and she could hear the strains of Schubert's *Rosamunde* floating out. Gilly must have put on a record. It was very sweet of her, and Lesley felt really touched as she went inside.

But it was Grenville and not Gilly who rose from the sofa and came to meet her. To Lesley's dismay, Gilly was not there at all.

'May I once more wish you a happy birthday, Lesley,' he said formally. He took a small tissue-wrapped parcel from his pocket. 'Here's a little gift that I hope you will accept.'

Lesley flushed deeply. 'There was no need,' she murmured, deeply embarrassed. He put the small packet into her hand and she looked up and met his quizzical dark grey glance. His hand closed about hers and he drew her firmly towards him. The light from the standard lamp by the record player lit one side of his face, though the other was in shadow, and Lesley could see the fine lines around his eyes and at the side of his mouth, and then that mouth touched her own lightly in a birthday kiss. In a second, it was no longer a birthday kiss – a kiss to go with a gift. It was a kiss that had got more than a little out of hand, and they drew apart abruptly. Lesley felt as if a flame had burned her lips. She was tinglingly aware of the strong physical attraction this man had for her. And though she looked at it cerebrally, yet the pulse at her temples still beat faster and the colour rose again in her cheeks.

There should be something for her to say, but she could think of nothing while he continued to look into her face. She wondered wildly, 'Is this an apology for having been so hard on me – and because he suspects that I'm going to have to surrender?' But he could have made it a vastly less personal gesture than a kiss on the lips that changed from a mere brush to a slightly mad and electrifying contact.

Firmly she released her hand from his.

'Thank you for the kiss! I must see what else you've given me.'

His lips twisted. 'It's nothing.'

'It's something,' contradicted Lesley lightly. 'My one and only gift.' She looked at him quickly. She shouldn't have said that – now he would ask hadn't Guy sent her anything. But he didn't, he merely looked back at her, his eyes narrowed, speculative.

She unwrapped her gift slowly. It was a silvery bracelet about an inch wide, made in an intricate flower design. In the centre of each silver flower was a small oval stone the colour of a turquoise. The fine clasp was safeguarded by a silver chain, and Lesley occupied herself in unfastening it. Her heart was hammering and she felt completely taken aback. How could he possibly have obtained a bracelet like this at a moment's notice? She was sure there was no such thing to be had in any of the shops at Balgola Bay. And why should he make her such a gift?

She raised her eyes to his.

'It's very beautiful, but—'

'But what? Don't you like it?' he asked, almost coldly.

'Of course I like it. But – there was no need for it—'

'Is there ever any need for a gift? I thought it might give you some pleasure. It's nothing of any consequence – a trinket I picked up in Istanbul some years ago when I was on my way home from study abroad . . . Are you going to put it on?'

'Of course,' said Lesley shakily. But her fingers seemed too clumsy to deal with the clasp and after a moment he took it from her, opened it, and enclosed it around her wrist.

'Your skin is made for gold rather than silver,' he said, his head bent, his cheek close to her hair. 'You're so very fair.'

Lesley watched his fingers – long and skilful and flexible as they dealt expertly with the fine clasp. He straightened and turned his head as Sister Gilbert appeared at the door.

She too carried a gift – a large flat parcel, wrapped in brown paper. Obviously a book.

'For you, Lesley, with my best love . . . Have you poured the sherry, Grenville?'

Lesley found she had to sit down. Her legs had suddenly become quite unreliable. She made for the couch. The Schubert music had come to an end, and a

Chopin waltz had begun. She told Gilly, 'Dr. Garrison's given me this beautiful bracelet. I feel terrible—'

'Don't be gauche, Lesley. You're twenty-one and a pretty girl, and you should be able to accept gifts with equanimity – as your due. Isn't that so, Gren?'

But Grenville had gone to the cabinet and was pouring the sherry, and asked over his shoulder as if he had not heard, 'What's that, Gilly?' And to Lesley's relief, she did not repeat her question.

Sister Gilbert's gift was a book on Australian gardens. 'I hope it will be useful when you start one of your own, Lesley.'

'It's terrific,' said Lesley, turning the pages. 'I'm going to enjoy just looking at it. How lucky I am!'

'It's good to see you happy.' Gilly raised her sherry glass. 'Here's to the birthday girl.'

They drank to her and Lesley raised her own glass. 'To – to Gilly and Dr. Garrison.'

'Better make it Grenville,' said Gilly. 'How can we go out and enjoy ourselves together at Joe's Mermaid Inn if you're going to be so formal?'

Lesley's heart lurched. Her eyes went to the man who was watching her nonchalantly across the room. So Grenville was coming to her birthday party! But of course – he had given orders that Gilly was not to exert herself with a lot of fancy cooking. It would be to save her trouble rather than for any other reason and perhaps she had insisted that he come too. And quite definitely he would be footing the bill. Lesley was not altogether sure that she liked that. It put her at a disadvantage to accept his favours. She had already and far too easily accepted the 'trinket' that he had clasped around her wrist. She looked at him warily, almost with distrust, and he looked back at her half amused.

'Yes, please forget the formality, Lesley.' His eyebrows tilted slightly, mockingly, and Lesley thought, 'What else could he say?' But even so, she didn't think she would be able to bring herself to call him Grenville.

He was about to close the front door behind them as they went out when the telephone rang and Gilly stepped back inside to answer it. Lesley stood with Grenville on the verandah waiting for her. It was a beautiful night, the air warm and soft and still, the sky huge and starry. A hazy golden moon rose from the sea, scattering light on the blackness of the ocean. Neither she nor Grenville said a word, but the sea filled the silence with a soft wooing murmur.

When Gilly rejoined them she wore a comical expression.

'Wouldn't such a thing happen tonight! Jenny Riley's broken her wrist and wants me to go over and put her mother to bed.'

'And you said yes?'

'I said no! I have no intention of missing my dinner.' Lesley, who had been holding her breath, relaxed. She was sure she couldn't possibly face dinner alone with Grenville Garrison. 'But,' said Gilly, 'I promised to go along at nine o'clock.'

The doctor linked his arm through hers affectionately.

'My Florence Nightingale – of course you did.'

Joe's Mermaid Inn turned out to be, as Lesley had suspected it would, that restaurant for lovers where Grenville had taken her once before. They ate steaks and they drank red wine – Gilly sparingly because she said it would never do to weave a tipsy way through Jenny Riley's houseful of treasures.

The Chinese pianist was playing again, and later a few couples went on to the tiny dance floor in the centre of the room, where they stood embracing rather than dancing. Lesley, lulled by the wine and the good food and the reassuring presence of Sister Gilbert, thought that it was a fantastic birthday after all. She glanced at her watch – it was a quarter to nine, nearly over.

'I shall have to go,' said Gilly, looking at her watch too. 'But you two stay here. I can take a taxi.' She stood up and so did Grenville, and Lesley, alarmed, got to her feet as well.

Grenville – she had not called him that yet, had avoided saying his name at all – put a casual hand on her arm. 'Sit down, Lesley. The night's not over yet.' She bit her lip and remained indecisive, met his eyes, and had to look away. 'There's still red wine in the bottle and music that is made for dancing. I'll be back with you in a minute.'

'Now sit down, Lesley – this is your night,' Sister Gilbert said, adding her insistence to his. She gave

Lesley one of her pleasant uncomplicated smiles and with a slight sigh the girl sat down. She watched the other two crossing the restaurant and had a sudden feeling of nervousness. She was crazy to stay here. It didn't matter that there was wine in the bottle, and the soft romantic piano music had nothing to do with her and Grenville Garrison. Nothing at all. In fact, when she came to consider it, Lesley couldn't imagine how in the world she came to be here tonight at all. If anyone had told her that it would happen again after that first time he had brought her here – in fact, if anyone had even suggested it to her last night, she would have been flatly disbelieving. Yet here she was.

And all it meant, she reminded herself presently, was that he was helping Gilly out, and perhaps was sorry for *her*, alone on her twenty-first birthday, and full of silly idealism about the sister who, she remembered she had told him, was not only beautiful but kind as well. He didn't believe that – not any more than Mr. Prescott or the hateful Mrs. Nelson. But tonight he was giving the silly girl a treat, coming back to drink more wine with her, to dance with her, to put the finishing touches to her evening.

She looked across at the dim and rosy lighting on the dance floor, at the couples who moved there, eyes closed, embracing. A restaurant for lovers. She positively could not dance with Grenville Garrison . . .

A moment later he came back to the table and stood looking down at her.

'Shall we dance, Lesley?'

She tilted her head. 'Dancing's not one of my things. You don't have to dance with me.'

He gave her a wry look. 'It's not one of my things either – but I think I could easily hold my own with the type of dancing that's being done here.'

Despite herself she smiled at that, and immediately his fingers closed around her wrist. 'We might as well be in it,' he said.

Lesley knew in no time that it had not been a good idea. Her instincts had been right – she ought to have resisted. The pianist sang a moody lyric, turned his head now and again to look with his liquid brown eyes straight at her and Grenville. Or so it seemed to Lesley, as they swayed together, dappled with romantic rose and violet lights, his arms about her, their bodies in casual but close contact.

'Girl, will you always be midnight to my noon?

Time like a waterwheel turning,

Moon vestal, sun burning, wheel turning . . .'

Vacuous words, yet they had a hypnotic effect. Lesley could feel her bones beginning to melt, she slipped into a kind of mental swoon, aware only of the man who held her in his arms, of the fact that he was a very, very attractive man in spite of everything . . . Close to him like this, her body was criss-crossed with the craziest feelings – the sharp pains of delight and desire went through her like knives, taking her breath and leaving her spent, almost gasping, weak as water. She felt herself slacken, and then in reaction tense nervously, and as if aware that something was disturbing her, he looked down at her and asked briefly, 'Had enough?'

'Enough,' she breathed.

He put his hand lightly on her waist and led her from the floor; looked at her pale face and told her, 'You need a breath of fresh air, Lesley. Too much wine and excitement. Collect your purse and your scarf—'

Lesley had a ridiculous feeling that she was about to be cheated of the rest of her evening with Grenville, and she collected her things with a strange unwillingness.

But once outside, she discovered that he had no intention of taking her home yet. There was evidently a graceful way of bringing the party to a close and he was taking it. A walk along the sand – a breath of air to clear her mind of the confusion caused by too much wine and too much excitement. And too much Grenville? wondered Lesley. It was an unedifying thought.

His hand firmly holding her bare arm just above the elbow, he escorted her across the narrow sloping strip of coarse grass and on to the beach. The moon, higher in the heavens now and paler, had scattered a trail of dancing silver flakes across the moaning sea, and the waves sighed against the shore.

They left the soft dry sand and walked in silence by the silvery-voiced, rhythmically moving sea, and now his arm was lightly and unnervingly around her waist. She wondered what he was thinking about. Certainly not her ... Of his drowned wife, perhaps, of some aspect of his life of which she knew nothing – of his personal life that rumour had it did not exist. Yet a man with Grenville Garrison's good looks and obvious virility must have a personal life.

Slowly, as they walked, Lesley reached a curious state of mindlessness. Nothing seemed to matter any more, nothing worried her. Her bemused eyes moved between the broken glitter of the water and the pale virginal moon that floated eerily over the sea.

'Girl, will you always be midnight to my noon?' The words of the song seemed to fit themselves to the lazy drugged swell of the ocean, and she began to hum the melody tentatively, then to put the words to it, her glance going to the profile of the man at her side – a profile turned aloofly from her as if he were unaware of her presence, of her voice, and thought of other things. They had reached the end of the small crescent of beach and were walking in the deep mysterious shadows of a thick grove of tea trees.

'Moon vestal, sun burning, wheel turning,' sang Lesley huskily, and he turned suddenly, violently towards her. She heard his muttered exclamation, 'My God!' – and the rest of it was lost as she stumbled against a rock half buried in the sand and found herself in his arms. His lips were against hers in a kiss that was savagely passionate, his fingers caressed her nape, the curve of her throat, her bare shoulder. She clung to him, drowned in a sudden passion whose existence she had never before dreamed of – willing him not to let her go even though her breath had all but gone, leaving her half swooning against him.

And then, like a poisoned shaft, remembrance struck at her. 'Offering your kisses on the beach to a man who's looking for a little light sexual entertainment . . .' She freed herself almost viciously from his demanding arms, shocked, sickened. He thought she was that sort of a girl! And he – whatever his personal life or lack of it, whatever his godlike stature professionally – he was positively and aggressively masculine, a virile man with a man's needs, a man's compulsive desires.

'Don't!' She turned her face violently from him, thankful for the deep shadow, not wanting to step out into what now looked like glaring white moonlight on a stark white beach.

'I'm sorry.' His voice was harsh, taut. 'If you don't want such things to happen you should take care not to be so damned provocative.'

'Should I?' So it was all her fault, was it? Another adverse note in her dossier . . . 'Is that why you brought me here? To – to test me—' She almost said 'Tempt'.

'Be quiet,' he said roughly. 'You're not so childlike and ingenuous as to think that. Of course I shouldn't have brought you here. Equally, you should have had more sense than to invite me with that wanton voice of yours, those suggestive words, that erotic melody—'

Lesley gasped unbelievingly. He was accusing her of making a calculated attack upon his senses, his virtue! She thought of some of *his* actions this evening, when through *his* choice there had been physical contact at least verging upon the intimate between them. When he had, under cover of offering a birthday gift, first put his lips to hers – when he had more or less insisted that they should dance. Hadn't *he* been inviting *her* then – to a physical response that she knew was inadmissible? Her still hammering heart, her leaping pulses, her quivering nerves – the sensation of a palpable, visible kiss still lying upon her bruised lips, were testimony to her own wild response. But most certainly the blame for the passion that had flared between them lay mainly with him.

What was his object? she wondered wildly as by unspoken consent they began to walk back along the beach towards the softly-lit restaurant and the line of cars parked along the roadside.

This time they walked with a good eighteen inches between them, and it was some time before she could bring herself even to glance at him. Exactly how much did he know of what was happening within her physical and psychic being? Or did he see her uncomplicatedly as a girl with no depth, a girl who took her fun where she could find it, who regarded this kind of thing as – what had he said when they first met? –'a frivolous deviation'?

They had reached the car before he spoke, and his voice was low and controlled and infinitely distant.

'I shall be attending a medical conference in Sydney at the end of the week, Miss Brooke. I think you'd better take the opportunity and come with me. To rejoin your fiancé,' he added, as if it were necessary.

Lesley said jerkily, unevenly, 'Thank you. But I've

already arranged with Guy to go to Sydney on Saturday.'

'If you've booked your flight, cancel it,' he said almost savagely. 'To leave earlier can only be to your own advantage. And to your fiancé's delight.'

And for her to leave with him, she reflected cynically, would be an assurance that she did indeed leave – for that was what he wanted.

He opened the door of the car and let her into the front seat, went round and got in beside her.

'Take my advice and bring all your luggage with you. There's plenty of room in the boot and I think it highly probable that you will not be back. You've miscalculated your own needs in cutting yourself off from your lover as you have done.'

He started up the motor and they moved off and in the darkness her cheeks flamed. It was clear that her response to his kisses had jolted him quite as much as it had jolted her. And now she was labelled 'provocative'.

'I'll let you know what time to be ready on Friday morning,' he told her chillingly when he let her out of the car at Leura House. He had taken her silence for agreement with his plans. Lesley managed a stiff, 'Thank you,' and hoped he would take that to cover the whole of her abortive birthday celebrations. She slipped away quickly through the garden and went quietly to her room. She had no desire to encounter anyone just now.

In her bedroom she switched on the wall light and

stared at herself in the mirror as if at a stranger – at her wide, almost frightened, black-pupilled eyes, at her guilty lips that still seemed to wear that passionate, mad kiss.

What was happening to her?

CHAPTER SIX

THE next three days went by somehow. Lesley encountered Grenville Garrison in the ward several times. He was as attentive to, and as gentle with Jane as ever; pleasant to Lesley, but formal. Even less than formal. Cool. Distinctly cool. She was acutely aware of his complete personal withdrawal from her. It said clearly that she was not the type of girl he would ever select to adopt a child.

No more was said about his taking her to Sydney with him, but that was probably because he preferred to cut down contact with her to an absolute minimum.

She was sure that was the case when she returned to Leura House on Thursday evening to be told by Sister Gilbert, 'You've just missed Grenville, Lesley. He wants you to be ready at five-thirty in the morning. We'll certainly have to be on our toes, won't we?'

'Not you, Gilly.' Lesley managed a smile. 'I have no intention of disturbing your beauty sleep. I'll set my alarm clock – so please don't think you have to get up.'

She telephoned Guy that night, for she had not told him of her altered arrangements.

'Great,' he said. 'But you'll have to amuse yourself tomorrow, Lesley – I have a business luncheon.'

Lesley made a little face and absent-mindedly twisted her engagement ring around so that she could not see the pretty sapphire. It was a symbol that had lost its significance. She knew that engagements could be broken over the telephone and often were, and wondered if she should have dealt with her own that way. Possibly she would have, if she had not been so sure it would put her hopes of adopting Jane in jeopardy. She had done a lot of crooked thinking one way and another since she had arrived at Balgola Bay . . .

'Emma's flat is number eight,' Guy told her. 'Straight opposite mine. There's a flower box on the landing with some ferns and stuff in it. I'll get Emma to leave the key under that. Right?'

'Fine,' said Lesley.

'And don't forget your party gear, honey, for that date on Saturday night. We're going to have a mad and glorious weekend!'

Lesley's heart actually sank a little at his heartiness. She didn't feel terribly interested in a mad and glorious week-end. And she couldn't help observing that he took it for granted she was only visiting Sydney – not staying. Don't forget your party gear. It had been left for Grenville Garrison to regard her move as a permanent one.

She called in at the hospital before she went to bed, but she did not sleep well that night. Too many things were milling around in her mind. She had more than one good reason for this visit to Sydney. She would settle her relationship with Guy once and for all – and she had little real doubt as to which way it would be settled. As well, she was determined to bring back with her a reassured mind about the sister whom she had always loved and looked up to.

Of course she was coming back to the south coast. She had told Gilly that. She had to see Jane again even if finally she handed her over to the loving care of another woman. But she was not going to lose the battle easily.

She fell asleep at last, and it seemed only minutes later that the alarm clock rang and it was time to get up. She thought of dashing in to see Jane, but the child would still be asleep, and besides, she mustn't keep Grenville waiting. The nurses had assured her that everything would be fine while she was away. She wondered if Grenville had hinted that she might not be back, but it seemed he had not. 'That baby's on the mend now,' Nurse Warren had said the night before. 'She'll miss you, and she'll make a fuss and sulk, but I'll bet my bottom dollar she'll eat up all her dinner with a bit of wheedling, just the same. She's beginning to feel secure now, and to take an interest in the other kids.'

Grenville arrived at five-twenty-five. Lesley had sneaked out without waking Gilly and was waiting at the gate, her baggage beside her. She had brought everything, partly because at heart she was a little bit frightened of Grenville. He might send her back to pack up the remainder of her belongings if he suspected she had disobeyed what had been in the nature of an order!

'Is this all?' He sent her a quick searching glance as he stooped to pick up the two suitcases.

Lesley nodded. 'Everything.'

'Good.' While she climbed into the front seat he stowed the luggage in the back, and then they set off in silence.

Tense though she was at first, it was not long before she felt herself relaxing. The early morning air was fresh, though it rapidly grew warmer, and the coast with its tracts of bushland and forest looked clean and free from the ravages of man. A truce had evidently been called, for Grenville broke the silence occasionally to point out something he wanted her to see. Once it was a satin bower-bird stalking in the bush not ten feet from the road. Later he slowed the car down on a stretch of road that ran straight and narrow through a forest of tall eucalypts. Beneath the trees, the ground was green with ferns and native shrubs and Lesley could hear the sound of a creek and something else nearer at hand. Chink-chink-chink-chink — like the clear repeated ringing of tiny bells.

She looked questioningly at the man beside her.

'Bellbirds,' he said with a smile. 'I'll give you ten dollars if you can catch sight of one of them, Lesley.' He actually pulled up and let her out of the car, and she crept forward stealthily and stood for perhaps five minutes watching and listening, while back in the car he smoked a cigarette. The bell-like chimes continued, moving mysteriously away and then returning, but stare though she might Lesley couldn't glimpse even a feather and she was forced to give up. They smiled at each other a little warily before they set off again, and it occurred to her that it was strange they could behave like this, as if nothing – dangerous had sprung up between them only a few nights ago. Their truce evidently entailed a diplomatic silence about what had happened and should not have happened. But it was there in Lesley's mind just the same, and she was sure it must be in his too, not far from the surface.

She started almost with fear when he said her name not many minutes later.

'Lesley—'

'Here it comes,' she thought. 'He's going to bring it back into the open.'

But of course he wasn't. He asked her austerely, 'Are you going to take the advice I gave you the other day and forget about your sister's neighbours?'

Lesley felt her heartbeats slow down almost to normal again, though her cheeks were still stained with pink.

'I'm sorry, but I'm not.'

'I wish you would,' he said firmly. 'People change, you know.'

Yes, Lesley knew very well that people changed. She had changed – Guy had changed. She said, 'But not – not radically – not as from other people's accounts my sister must have changed. Not as much as that.'

'As much as that and even more,' he contradicted her. 'Sometimes it can happen after childbirth – or after some illness, or an accident. A woman can suffer what is virtually a complete change of personality.'

Lesley shook her head. 'Not Linda.'

She saw a look of impatience cross his handsome face. 'It can happen to anyone,' he said shortly. 'Even to those we love the most.'

Lesley bit her lip to restrain herself from an angry outburst. 'You never knew my sister. She was – she was dead before you'd ever heard of her. So what grounds have you for implying that she was different from the way I remember her?'

He sighed wearily. 'All right, go your own way. But if you get hurt, don't be surprised. I've given you what I consider good advice. Ignore it if you must.'

'I have been hurt already. And – I must,' said Lesley. 'I mean to go to Cremorne this afternoon. If you like, I shall give you a full report on the result of my investigations when next we meet.'

'There'll be no need for that.' He sounded sorry for her. He added, 'And when will that be?'

Lesley gave him a blank stubborn look. 'Next week. At the hospital.'

'You're so sure you'll be back? So sure you'll persuade your fiancé? I don't want you back on other terms, you know.'

Lesley turned her head to look out of the window. He didn't want her back at all. She would stay in Sydney if he had his way.

'I'll be back,' she said.

'I shall ring you before I leave. If you're coming, you might as well come with me.'

When they reached the outskirts of the city a couple of hours later, the sun had gone, the sky was overcast, and it was beginning to rain, though the air was hot and steamy and breathless. It was the first rain she had seen since leaving England.

'Where are you staying?' he asked her, and she saw his lips curve in a sardonic smile when she gave him Guy's address.

'Before you jump to conclusions,' she followed up quickly, 'I shan't be staying in Guy's flat, but with a – a friend in the apartment opposite.'

No comment!

At Kirribilli, despite the rain or perhaps because of it, he insisted on coming upstairs with her. There was an elevator, and she assured him that there was no need. 'Besides – your conference.'

'That takes place after lunch.'

He was so grimly determined that Lesley was sure he must expect the worst.

'Another check? Another entry in my file?' she asked with a lift of her fine eyebrows. He was not amused and looked at her with a fiery impatience in his dark eyes.

'Think what you like,' he said forbiddingly.

Lesley had been in this building only once before – on the morning of her arrival in Sydney – and then she had gone straight to Guy's flat while he broke the news about the Jarmyns to her. She had not ever been in Emma's flat, but it was number eight, and she had her instructions about finding the key under the flowerpot, and this she did without fumbling. Meanwhile, Grenville set her bags down in front of the door to number eight, and when Lesley turned with the key in her hand she found him watching her with a very odd expression on his face – puzzled, thoughtful, speculative.

She had put the key in the lock before she discovered the probable cause of that look. It was the small framed card below the shining silver figure eight.

EMMA BURKE.

Lesley's face flamed with sudden guilty colour that ebbed quickly, leaving her pallid and shaken. So Emma was the girl who had been out dancing with Guy, who had rung the hospital and left a message for Dr. Garrison that she would be down as soon as she could! Who had caused Lesley such a load of trouble that she now considered might have been, in the long run, totally unnecessary.

She turned the key and pushed open the door and Grenville went inside with her luggage.

'Where do you want these, Lesley?' His dark eyes had not by any means lost their speculative look, though there was something grim about them now. Obviously he was trying to fit all the pieces together. If Guy had been playing around with some other girl, then where had Lesley been? As to whether Lesley knew – her telltale colour must have revealed to him as plainly as words that it was a big surprise to her as it was to him to see that name on the door.

Never having been here in her life, she didn't know where her luggage should go – whether there were two bedrooms or only one. She told him casually, 'Don't

117

worry about them – in the hall will do. And – and thank you very much for the lift and for your trouble, Dr. Garrison.'

A wry smile touched his lips. 'Am I not to be offered a cup of coffee? I've told you I'm in no great hurry.'

Lesley looked back at him hopelessly. She supposed that in a way it had been gentlemanly of him to make no comment on the name on the door, but if he stayed for coffee, was his chivalrous silence going to continue? She hardly thought so. She didn't think there was much point in further explorations into her or Guy's characters in his view – she had lost her cause long ago, only she was too stubborn to give in. She heard herself say weakly, 'Yes, of course you must have some coffee.' She closed the door and looked around her for the first time, curious herself about Emma Burke – who might yet turn out to be a middle-aged spinster rather than a dangerous bachelor girl.

Somehow Lesley didn't think that would be so. Not after a quick look at the flat.

A big living-room opened off the hallway, and she took Grenville there. The big windows made it full of light despite the rainy day. There were white sheepskin rugs scattered over charcoal grey wall-to-wall carpeting – rugs that looked as if they would be wonderful to lie about on – and the furniture was old but painted up in true decorator style in clear blues and sour greens. There was a huge abstract painting on one wall, and on a small table by the windows that looked, like Guy's, over the harbour, a large white card was propped up against a pewter mug stuffed with big yellow paper poppies. 'Hi, Lesley! Make yourself at home! Yours is the bed furthest from the window. I shan't be home tonight, but hope we meet some time before you go.' It could be read from six feet away, so Grenville could have read it too and no doubt had. Well, it would tell him nothing, beyond what it told her. That Emma was bright and breezy and undoubtedly young to match her apartment.

She said, 'Please sit down. I'll get some coffee.'

It took her a while to find her way around the neat kitchen and she deliberately suspended thought. There was a percolator, but she decided to settle for instant coffee and put the electric kettle on. While it was heating she found sliced bread and made toast in a shining reflector toaster, then buttered it generously and piled it on a big plate. Emma Burke must have a good job. She had all sorts of kitchen gadgets, there was plenty of food in the refrigerator and a wooden wine rack in a cupboard held half a dozen bottles of wine. The cups and saucers were made of fine but plain china and not one of them had a crack in it. There were gay coffee mugs too, and Lesley put two of those on a tray that was patterned with stencilled flowers, added a pot of marmalade, milk and sugar and a big jug of coffee. As she carried it into the sitting-room, she reflected that it was like preparing an offering for the gods – hoping for mercy. But somehow she didn't expect mercy.

Grenville was standing at the window with his back to the room and she set the tray down on a long low table and joined him. There was a beautiful view of the harbour, whose waters lapped against a stone wall and a small wooden wharf just below the apartment block. The rain had stopped, but the sky was overcast and outlines were misty, colours muted. The harbour, that had been a sparkling blue last time she had seen it, was a misty silver grey. She could see the white-sailed roof of the Opera House rising from Benelong Point, and the small ferries that went to and fro from Circular Quay. And there was the soft green of the Botanic Gardens contrasting with the flimsy, transparent-looking skyscrapers whose glass walls reflected the ghostly gleam of the rainy day.

'You're a lucky girl, Lesley, if Guy's flat has a view like this,' Grenville said. 'It must be quite spectacular on a sunny day. But it's no place for a small child.'

Lesley agreed, but didn't say so. You couldn't bring a two-year-old to live in an apartment like this one. She turned from the window, poured the coffee, offered him toast and marmalade.

Presently he asked her casually, 'How long have you been engaged, Lesley?'

'Over two years,' she said, and saw his look of surprise at her answer.

'I see. And how long have you and your fiancé been in Australia?'

'Guy has been here a while longer than I have,' she answered evasively.

'And you?'

'A few – weeks,' she managed.

'Exactly how long?' he insisted, his eyes calculating.

'Not – not very long,' she stammered.

'You arrived – when?'

She gave in. 'The day I came to Balgola Bay.'

He pondered on that, and no doubt too he pondered about Miss Burke. Lesley hoped she would not be asked any questions about *her*, because she knew no more than he did.

'What kept you from coming out from England together?' he wanted to know next. He reached for the toast and dealt with a slice while she told him briefly about the grandmother who had brought her up and how she had stayed to look after her.

'There was no one else?'

She shook her head. 'Linda was married and she and Tony had arranged to come to Australia. We – Guy and I – didn't expect it to be so long before I was able to come.'

'And how long was it?'

'Two years.' Now he had forced it all out of her, now he must be wondering how well – or otherwise – their love had stood the test of time.

'I see.' He picked up the coffee jug. 'May I help myself?'

'Please do.' She glanced at the windows, the rain had begun again, heavy rain, and the room had darkened dramatically.

'He's waited for you a long time, this fiancé of yours, Lesley – even if he hasn't always waited alone.'

121

Lesley's colour rose. 'Whatever you mean by that, it isn't true. I mean,' she floundered, seeing the mocking amusement on his face at her outrageously sweeping statement, 'I mean, Emma Burke is a – is a mutual friend.'

His dark eyebrows rose. 'Really? You knew her in England, I take it.'

'No – I—'

'Then,' he said reasonably, 'I find it hard to believe you – since you admit to having come to Balgola Bay practically five minutes after you hit Sydney.'

Lesley bit her lip. 'Whatever you suspect about Emma and Guy it's not true,' she told him coldly. 'You jump to the worst conclusions just because for some reason or other you're determined to stop me from having Jane. Guy and I are not immoral monsters.'

A glint of amusement appeared fleetingly in his dark eyes.

'Have I ever suggested you were?'

'Maybe you have,' said Lesley. 'I know what you suspected that night you saw me on the beach with Bob Prescott. But if you knew the truth – I hadn't let him so much as kiss me, even though he wanted it.' She stood up and began feverishly to pack up the tray, and he rose too and she could feel him watching her. As if compelled, she looked up. His gaze was intent, purposeful and he had moved closer to her.

'Are you hoping to persuade me that you're not – susceptible, Miss Brooke?'

She stared at him. Her lips formed the words, 'Why

not?' but they were only just audible.

'Here's why not.'

One more step towards her and he had dragged her against the hardness of his body and was kissing her cruelly. Lesley fought back for three seconds and then it was as if she had fallen into the sea and the waters had closed over her head. She was no longer capable of resistance. Something in her even revelled in the savagery of his embrace – accepted it, responded to it. She clung to him drowningly.

He had actually to disentangle himself from her clinging arms to break free of her.

It was a shattering experience for Lesley and it revealed to her with blinding clarity something that she had no wish to know. She had fallen in love with Grenville Garrison. Otherwise she could never have answered to his passion as she had. She turned her face away from him, dreading that he might read in her eyes what she had only now discovered for herself.

'You're certainly no ice maiden, Lesley,' he said, his voice harsh and uneven. 'But just don't use that formidable combination of a face like that of a Botticelli angel and a stunningly passionate nature to blackmail your fiancé into doing what you want. For ultimately, that's the form your persuasion's going to take.'

'Is it? You couldn't be more wrong,' she breathed, conscious still of the mad racing of her blood and of the fire in her eyes.

'I couldn't be more right. And I can see nothing but disaster for a child brought up in a marriage contracted under those circumstances.'

'I wish,' said Lesley, red-cheeked, 'that you would mind your own business, and – and keep our relationship strictly impersonal in future.'

'I hope our *relationship*, as you call it,' he countered, his nostrils whitening, 'has about reached its end. I shall certainly not take you back with me to Balgola Bay.'

'Then I shall take the plane,' she flung at him, and she was quite determined that she would. It was more than doubtful that she would ever be able to adopt Jane permanently, and yet some obstinacy – or was it some instinct, some streak of the fey in her nature – made her determined to hang on. It was as if something outside her conscious knowledge was telling her what she must do. She only hoped it was not a sort of rationalization of this crazy attraction she felt towards Grenville Garrison.

She stooped once more and began to gather the coffee mugs, the sugar basin, and replace them on the tray. He watched her, unmoving, eyes narrowed, jaw set in anger or irritation, she did not know which, until she raised her head and said pointedly and rudely, 'You've had your coffee.'

He swung about and left her, and in a moment she heard the front door open and close.

Her nerves were jumping and her mind was seething. What a blow-up that had been! There had always, right from the first, been friction between them, though it sometimes retreated to well below the surface. Now that very friction seemed suspect, and she seemed to have lost her sense of direction entirely. She couldn't think what she was doing here in Emma Burke's flat — why she had let herself be persuaded to come to Sydney, what she was going to do about Guy and Jane. Just now, her one and only object appeared to have been to score a point over Grenville Garrison — even though he was perfectly right about Jane. Except, of course, that she would never use her physical person as a form of coercion in any way at all ... Despite her angry statement that she would take the plane to Balgola Bay, she soon began to wonder if she would have to back down. Yet how could she, now? And wasn't there still this conviction, reasonless, illogical but nevertheless undeniable, that she must not give in? Not yet!

With a sudden grimace and a deep sigh, she decided to shelve her problems for a while. She carried the tray out to the kitchen and washed the crockery and silver that she had used, brushed away crumbs from the counter top, found a pretty broom in a cupboard and swept the floor, then went to inspect the bedroom. There, she lay flat on her back on the bed near the window — a bed that was really a divan, piled with cushions — and tried to relax.

As she lay there, the conviction grew on her that she liked Emma Burke. This was a personality room, decorated in ivory and orange with a touch of acid green, and it was not over-tidy. Emma had left some of her clothes lying about, and a fashion magazine lay open on the floor. Another abstract painting, rather smaller than the one in the living-room, made a splash of colour on the wall. Rather disappointingly there were no photographs.

Soon Lesley's eyes closed and she slept for a while.

There is nothing as exhausting as emotion, she reflected when she woke again. It was still raining, and when she went to the living-room windows to look out, she saw a small ferry boat pull in to the wharf below, wait while a few passengers came aboard, then head back towards Circular Quay. Lesley went back to the bedroom, changed into a sleeveless navy and white town dress, donned her white all-weather coat, tied a waterproof scarf over her hair and left the apartment.

She walked down to the wharf and after a wait of five or six minutes caught a ferry. She stood under shelter at the back, watching the grey-green water, and the spray flying to mingle with the rain. She refused to allow her mind to return to the scene she had enacted with Grenville. It was too disturbing. She was going to Cremorne to find the apartment where Linda had lived and she would concentrate on doing just that.

It was a peaceful and beautiful ride across the harbour, and she was pleased to discover there was another ferry trip ahead of her to Cremorne – this time on a larger ferry, but one not nearly as large as those that made the seven-mile journey across the Heads to Manly.

From the wharf at Cremorne, she walked in thinning rain along a narrow path sheltered by gum trees that smelt freshly of eucalyptus in the damp steamy air. She crossed a tiny bridge over a gully where blue morning glories cascaded and brown water tumbled along, and was presently in the street where Linda had lived for a while with Tony and Jane. The block of flats, when she found it, proved to be quite unlike the smart modern building at Kirribilli.

It was an old place, the woodwork needed painting and the garden was running wild. Lesley thought it must once have been a big home, a single dwelling, since converted to flats. Linda had mentioned living on the ground floor, but all the downstairs windows were closed and Lesley hurried through the rain up a sloping ramp that led to a covered porch and an upstairs flat. While she waited for her ring to be answered, she looked down into the gully below. There was a grassy reserve, fringed with bottlebrush and small eucalypts, and she thought it was a pleasant area, even though the house was old and shabby. A good place for children.

The woman who came to the door had prematurely white hair, blue eyes, and a delicate and unlined face.

'Yes? Is it about board?'

Lesley said with a pleasant smile that it wasn't about board.

'I wanted to ask about some people who lived here a short while ago – the Jarmyns.'

'You're trying to trace them?' the woman asked, her

eyes wary.

'No. I know about the accident. Mrs. Jarmyn was my sister.'

'Oh.' Hand on the door knob, she waited. Lesley had hoped that she might be more friendly and ask her inside.

'I arrived from England only recently, hoping to see my sister again. You must have known her.'

'Yes, I knew her. But not terribly well. They were here less than three months.'

It was hard going, but Lesley said determinedly, 'Could I talk to you a little about my sister, please?'

The woman hesitated, then said, 'Come along inside.' She led the way to an old-fashioned room whose narrow windows looked into the rainy bush, and motioned Lesley to a shabby armchair. 'I own these flats. My name is Fairweather, Kathleen Fairweather. And you are—?'

'Lesley Brooke.'

'You have your sister's eyes,' said Mrs. Fairweather consideringly. She sat on the edge of another armchair as if she were determined not to be there for long. 'But you're a real blonde. Mrs. Jarmyn was a lot darker.' She paused for a second. 'I'll set your mind at rest. They didn't owe me any money. Almost everyone else you could think of, but not me. In fact, they'd paid the rent for a week longer than they stayed.' She glanced at the window, then back at Lesley. 'And Mrs. Jarmyn's engagement ring – I suppose you're wondering what became of that. I can tell you. She sold it to pay the rent – not that I pressed her, you understand. She sold other things too, I daresay. But that was her business – not for me to interfere in her financial problems.'

She stopped speaking and looked at Lesley rather uneasily as if she didn't like talking about these things. Lesley was used by now to the fact that the Jarmyns had been in debt, but it sounded like the Linda she had known to make an effort to pay her bills, though it was sad to think she had had to pawn or sell her personal jewellery to do so. Certainly she and her grandmother appeared to have been right in not caring particularly for Tony. He hardly seemed to have been a good provider.

She said slowly, 'Yes, she certainly had problems. I wonder if you know where I could find any of her friends?'

'She didn't have friends,' said the woman with a shrug. 'Not that I know of. She looked after the baby, took her for walks, kept the flat neat and tidy – did her shopping. Kept herself to herself. Now he was different, he had a lot of friends, though I couldn't tell you who they were. He was always out, hardly ever in to a meal – away a good deal of the time too. I don't know where he went, I suppose it was business, she never told me. It was lonely for her. I used to wonder how a quiet girl like that came to marry a man like him. No idea of doing anything with his money other than spend it on the pleasures of the senses – he had that look in his eye. I was sorry for her.'

'Yes,' said Lesley slowly. 'It can't have been easy.'

She reflected that Mrs. Fairweather at least didn't seem to regard Linda as having been a good-time girl. 'I don't think she can have been very happy.'

'No more do I. Though she'd never hear a word of criticism about him. Still in love, I suppose – it's a funny old world, isn't it? I was surprised when they left. He'd gone away somewhere on his own, and I went to spend a few days with my sister in Parramatta. When I came back they'd gone – without a word. And next day I heard about the accident.' She paused for breath. 'How is the baby? I read somewhere that she was in a bad state.'

'She's better now, thank you,' said Lesley, and after a moment asked bluntly, 'Mrs. Fairweather, did my sister – drink much?'

The woman looked genuinely surprised. 'Drink? Dear me no, never anything like that. Sick, she often looked sick, she wasn't a strong-looking girl, but she didn't drink and she didn't take drugs, no matter what her worries. I had a girl here once who took drugs and I know the signs . . . No, Mrs. Jarmyn was so wrapped up in that child of hers she'd never have taken anything that would impair her efficiency. I remember one morning little Jane toddled off while she was washing her hair – got into the baker's van. Your sister was demented till she'd found her again. She was very quiet, a very nice girl.' She looked at Lesley questioningly. 'Was there anything else?'

Lesley shook her head. She had heard, more or less, what she had wanted to hear, yet somehow she was not really happy with it. Still – 'Thank you very much for giving me your time, Mrs. Fairweather,' she said, getting up from her chair.

'You're welcome.' The woman rose too and walked with her to the door. She appeared to be having a slight inner struggle. She said finally, 'I have a little confession to make, Miss Brooke. Your sister left a few of her personal belongings, and some of the baby's, when she went. I didn't say anything to the police – it was an unpleasant business to be mixed up in. I just explained that the Jarmyns had left while I was away, that the rent had been paid and that I knew they were going to Melbourne. I didn't know actually, but it saved a lot of fuss and bother and questioning. If I'd known you were coming I'd have kept the things for you, but I gave them away – to the Aboriginal Welfare Society. There was nothing of value—'

'It can't be helped,' said Lesley. She felt cold. Mrs. Fairweather had opened the door and rain was still falling and the day looked cheerless. She thought it strange that Linda should have left anything behind – particularly when she was apparently short of money. Strange too that she and Tony should have departed so suddenly—

They shook hands and she said good-bye, and made her way to the ferry, head down against the rain. Grenville had been in some degree quite wrong in advising her against coming here. True, she had heard things that had saddened her, but she was absolutely certain now that all the other hints and suggestions, the snap character sketches she had been offered, were wrong, off centre. Linda had remained still the girl she had known.

Yet where did it all get her? Her sister was still gone . . .

CHAPTER SEVEN

In all, Lesley was disturbed and more than a little puzzled by her visit to Mrs. Fairweather. Yet at least her sister had been presented more or less as the person she remembered. She had ceased to be shocked by the fact that the Jarmyns were always in debt, though it was unnerving to think that Linda had had to pawn her engagement ring to pay the rent. That was really sordid. And Tony – it was senseless to pretend otherwise – had been a charming scoundrel, and perhaps rather worse than a scoundrel.

The telephone was ringing in Emma Burke's flat as she groped under the pot plant for the key, and when she let herself in and answered it, it was Guy.

'Lesley, I've been trying to raise you half the afternoon. I began to think you'd decided not to come ... Look, I've got tickets for a show tonight. So put on your pretty clothes, grab an umbrella and come into town. We'll treat ourselves to dinner at King's Cross and enjoy ourselves in spite of this lousy weather.'

Lesley's spirits sagged. She would so much sooner have had a quiet evening at the flat. On the other hand, she was a little frightened at the thought of hours alone with Guy.

It was a superficially gay evening. They took a taxi to King's Cross, and she saw the glitter of the beautiful el Alamein fountain, the cosmopolitan crowds, the to-ing and fro-ing that went on madly, incessantly, despite the rain. They ate in a crowded restaurant where they had a table too close to the orchestra to make intimate talk — or any sort of talk at all, come to that — possible. There were a pianist, a guitarist and a drummer, also a singer with very powerful vocal chords who sang the latest hits. Guy really set himself out to give Lesley a good time, but the trouble was he was completely out of touch with her taste in good times, and she found it all distinctly nerve-racking.

The show they went to was a bedroom comedy, a little vulgar, but funny and sophisticated, lighthearted and ridiculous. The audience, including Guy, loved it. Afterwards they took a taxi home across the harbour bridge. The rain had disappeared, the sky was miraculously clear and starry above the glare of the city, and Guy put his arm around Lesley and asked her if she thought she would like Sydney.

'It's a terrific place to live. You'll have an entirely wrong view of Australia if you judge it by a country town like Balgola Bay.'

At Kirribilli, she begged to be excused from coming in for a nightcap and meeting Douglas Potter, who was in the flat and apparently not alone. She unlocked the door to Emma's flat feeling weary and wrung out, and Guy came inside with her to kiss her good night.

That kiss told her a lot. She knew a strange inner shrinking and reluctance, as though she were being kissed by a complete stranger. It was not, as Guy half-laughingly suggested it must be, the fact that she was unused to his moustache that made her so timid. To Lesley, it was grimly revealing that she should be so unresponsive when with Grenville Garrison she had completely lost her head.

When they finally parted for the night she felt relieved. The evening had been like a giant soap bubble – glittering and bouncing and pretty, and utterly ephemeral. It had vanished without a trace . . .

They had a late breakfast the following morning in his flat. The rain had gone, the sky was a brilliant blue with not a cloud in sight, the harbour was dazzlingly beautiful in the summer sunshine.

'It's going to be a scorching day,' said Guy with satisfaction. 'Just what I was hoping for. We'll drive up to one of the northern beaches. How does Collaroy sound?'

'It sounds wonderful,' said Lesley, who didn't know one beach from another. She sipped her grapefruit juice and drew a deep breath. There had to be some time for serious talk between herself and Guy, and for a start she was going to solve the mystery of Miss Burke – Emma Burke. She looked across the table at the man sitting opposite her – hazel-eyed, moustached, suntanned, much heavier than he used to be. It was downright frightening to think that she had promised to marry him. He looked back at her with open admiration in his eyes, and involuntarily she recalled Grenville's remarks about her – 'a face like that of a Botticelli angel'.

'Guy,' she began hesitantly, 'it's wonderful I can have that flat. I hope I haven't driven Emma away by turning up.'

'Of course you haven't, honey. Emma's not like that. Everything's okay, just don't worry.'

'Tell me about her.'

He reached across to switch off the pop-up toaster. 'Tell you what?' he said casually. 'She's a great girl – a fashion artist, a career girl.'

'Is she by any chance the girl you got to fill in for me on that Hawkesbury River trip, Guy?'

He looked at her in surprise, his expression suddenly closed. 'As a matter of fact, she is. She got back from her holiday in the nick of time, which was a bit of luck for me. Got me out of a nasty spot.'

'Emma *Burke*,' said Lesley slowly. Then just as she was preparing to launch into the story of how she had been called Miss Burke at the Balgola Bay Hospital, Douglas Potter appeared. And that was the end of that.

He was an extrovert young man, fair-haired and blue-eyed, as sun-tanned as Guy, and curious to meet Lesley – 'the girl we've all heard so much about.'

'You must be a paragon, Lesley,' he said, examining her frankly. 'I hope you'll stay around long enough to prove it to us.'

Was that a sly dig at her for moving out before she had even moved in? Lesley suspected it was, and decided that she would not make up her mind yet whether she liked him or not. She had plenty of time during the day to decide, however, because he and his girl-friend Madeleine came to the beach too, in Guy's car.

It was a day as hectic in its way as last night had been a hectic evening – the radio on in the car, red-haired Madeleine talking non-stop, making a fuss about the price she had paid for eye make-up that had smudged, asking did they *have* to go to Collaroy. Finally, owing to her pressure, they went to a beach much further north – Palm Beach, which was smarter and more sophisticated than Collaroy, it seemed. Without the noise, Lesley could have enjoyed better the long and beautiful drive past a succession of golden-sanded beaches strung out along the coast. At Palm Beach they ran into people they knew, and Lesley felt herself something of an outsider. It was a long day – a day spent lying about on the sand, or sitting at tables in outdoor restaurants drinking or eating, and all the time the talk went on. Lesley didn't know if she was on her head or her heels. She hadn't much in common with Madeleine, who appeared to be more interested in clothes than anything else, and she had the distinct and uneasy feeling that Douglas Potter didn't like her. He taxed her several times with being too quiet.

'We thought you were going to be quite a girl.'

That was the phrase Mr. Prescott had chosen to describe Linda, and Lesley didn't think it could ever have applied either to her or to her sister. She fancied that Guy was disappointed in her 'performance' – in the impression she was creating. He would have liked her to shine. And though he apparently found Douglas Potter's needling irritating too, it was obviously not for the same reason that Lesley found it so. The notion occurred to her that Guy was trying to fit her into a kind of life that did not appeal to her. Had he forgotten what she was really like? Had he, during the time they were parted, dreamed her up into a different sort of person? And was he now expecting her to *be* that kind person – extrovert, 'quite a girl' – and disappointed that she had let him down?

Back at the Kirribilli flat late in the afternoon he presented her with his birthday gift – an enormous bottle of the French perfume that was her favourite. At least he had remembered that, and she was touched, as she accepted it and the kiss that accompanied it. Her birthday, as had previously been planned, was to be celebrated that night, and Douglas Potter and Madeleine were joining the party. In Emma's flat, Lesley showered and washed her hair and dried it with Emma's hair drier. She got into a bare-shouldered simply cut short dress that was the colour of a damask rose, a deep and velvety red, and pinned her shining hair up in a loop, leaving a curling tendril to fall softly at each side of her face. She made lavish use of the French perfume and then, on some silly impulse, clasped the bracelet that Grenville Garrison had given her about her arm. After all, he had said it was just a trinket, and she might as well wear it, since she had accepted it. Besides – But then her mind went conveniently blank.

138

They went to a colourful and informal Spanish restaurant in the city where Guy had reserved a table for four. Madeleine wore a showy green and gold pants dress with a very low neckline. Unlike Lesley, she had evidently not found time to wash the dulling salt water from her hair, for she was wearing an elaborately coiffed wig. Her jewellery consisted of primitive-looking copper ear-rings with a heavy necklet to match, and Lesley wondered if the other girl was over-dressed or if her own gear was just too simple. She was in no doubt as to what Douglas Potter thought, and she had a suspicion that Guy would have liked her to look more spectacular. This had the effect of putting her slightly on the defensive, which was unfortunate, but there it was. She wasn't like Madeleine and she had no intention of pretending that she was. All Madeleine's gestures were dramatic, her voice was just a shade too loud, her laughter theatrical, and she loved the lime-light.

There was a long discussion as to whether they should have Spanish wine or Australian, but as no agreement was reached, Madeleine insisting on one and the two men on the other, they started off with a bottle of each. And wine remained the topic of conversation until their dinner appeared, when they switched to food – and certainly the Spanish food was excellent, though it didn't help Lesley, who was beginning to feel tongue-tied. Madeleine, who had spent six weeks of the previous summer in Indonesia, with a group of students, was soon holding the floor with a dissertation on Indonesian dishes.

Later there was a floor show, with flamenco dancers who were good and music that was exciting.

More than once, Guy told Lesley, 'You're very quiet,' and though she felt guilty and unco-operative, she seemed to have become physically incapable of contributing more than a token share to the conversation. She did not shine at all.

When he took her on to the crowded dance floor and they stood close together with his arms around her, her mind went of its own accord to her other birthday party and her dance with Grenville – a dance that had, in its way, started off a lot of fireworks. Guy bent his head to hers to talk lightly about nothing – 'You smell delicious. And you look like an angel with that shining fair hair.'

'A Botticelli angel?' she asked wryly.

He looked slightly wounded at this reception to his compliment. 'I don't know – any sort of an angel.'

And then a girl whose long black hair fell half across her face grabbed him by the arm and said, 'Hi, darling, where's Emma tonight?'

'I wouldn't know,' said Guy. He smiled, but he said it shortly, and he manoeuvred Lesley away from that particular part of the dance floor.

Lesley, feeling a little sorry for him, asked brightly, 'Who was that?'

He shrugged. 'Some bird I met somewhere or other.'

'On the motor cruiser on the Hawkesbury,' suggested Lesley kindly.

'Maybe.' He held her closely and said no more.

Later, she danced with Douglas, though she did so reluctantly. Some of the time he sang rather noisily, looking down at Lesley maliciously to see if she was annoyed, and some of the time he completely ignored her to indulge in badinage with someone he knew.

'I don't believe you like our kind of fun,' he remarked after another girl had joined them for what he called a 'love-in' for about sixty seconds. 'You have a rather too serious turn of mind for our crowd, I suspect.'

He sounded as if he were looking for an argument, and Lesley said bluntly, 'Why don't you like me, Douglas? For I'm quite aware that you don't.'

He didn't deny it. 'Let's say for a start that you're a bit of a let-down. Guy gave you such a big write-up. My God, we all expected you to be a sort of beautiful blonde young Elizabeth Taylor, voluptuous and exciting. But your feet barely touch the ground. You're not one little bit – earthy, are you? You've certainly got looks, but frankly, I wonder if Guy's been deluding himself.'

'Thank you.' Lesley felt faintly sick. She said, 'I'd like to sit down.'

'If you say so.'

They left the floor and went back to the table. Guy was dancing with Madeleine and Douglas lit a cigarette and poured wine into their glasses. As a matter of principle, Lesley didn't touch hers.

'You haven't met Emma Burke, have you?' he asked

presently. He asked it deliberately and Lesley's pulses hammered. Whatever she had to learn about Emma Burke, she didn't want Douglas Potter teaching it to her.

She said coolly, 'She's been very kind letting me use her flat. It's a lovely flat – full of personality.'

'Emma's full of personality too. She's a great girl – a career girl, she'll tell you, a hard-headed bachelor girl. But inside every hard-headed bachelor girl, in my experience, is a little woman looking for love and a home of her own. And Emma must be all of twenty-eight.'

'So,' said Lesley, pushing back her chair, 'if you'll excuse me, I'm going to the powder room.'

So Douglas thought Emma and not Lesley was the girl for Guy. And he was probably right, but it was not his business. Moreover, if Guy had been as sure as Douglas was, wouldn't he have written to Lesley in England and asked her to free him from his promise? She didn't think he had a heart so soft he couldn't have brought himself to do it. No, Guy was not like that. He had waited for Lesley because that was what he had wanted to do. Taking her time in the cloakroom over retouching her make-up, Lesley actually smiled into the mirror. Had he really been waiting for a voluptuous young blonde Elizabeth Taylor? She was quite certainly not that, but Guy hadn't yet brought himself around to accepting the fact. In one respect, she was a good step ahead of him. She knew he was not the man she had waited for. With a little help from her he would face the facts too. The only problem seemed to be to get him to herself for long enough to have a private and personal conversation.

They left the restaurant in the small hours of the morning. Douglas took Madeleine back to her flat in Paddington in a cab, and Guy and Lesley drove across the bridge to Kirribilli. It looked as though they were to have their moment of privacy at last.

'Coffee?' Guy asked her as they stepped out of the elevator. 'Or eggs and bacon? Or are you dead on your feet?'

She was, but she wasn't going to admit it. She had managed a catnap in the car, and it seemed to be a case of now or never, particularly as Guy had revealed that he had a round of golf to play in the morning – business again! She was certainly not going to chicken out, so she said firmly, 'Coffee, please.'

She could say what she had to say over coffee. Bacon and eggs would make too much of an inroad on the all too few hours of sleep Guy was going to manage anyhow.

The coffee was quickly made and they carried it into the sitting-room and sat down on the settee.

'Enjoy yourself today?' asked Guy.

'Yes, thank you.' Lesley cradled her cup in her hands and smiled at him faintly while she looked for a place to begin.

'Tell me about Emma, Guy.'

'What's all this about Emma? Who's been giving you ideas about her? I've told you all there is to tell. I've taken her out now and again, I like her, she's a career girl.' He spread his hands and looked mildly exasperated. 'That's all. Nothing for you to get upset about.'

'I'm not upset,' said Lesley levelly. 'That's the thing. Can't you honestly see, Guy – we've grown out of each other. It's as simple and as plain as that.' She looked at him squarely and he glanced away, frowning.

'It's not as simple as that. You just aren't acclimatized yet, Lesley.' He paused, seeking for words, and Lesley wondered what on earth being acclimatized had to do with it. 'You've incarcerated yourself down the coast – and you've temporarily lost your sting. I know quite well you didn't really enjoy yourself today, and I'm sorry about that, but it's because you haven't unwound yet. Everything will click back into place once you've got over the mother hen bit.'

'Maybe I'm not going to get over the mother hen bit.'

'Now don't be crazy. You can't take on that kid permanently and tie yourself down at the ripe old age of twenty-one. I simply won't allow it.'

He stopped and they stared at each other. Lesley put down her cup. 'I think you'd better take your ring back, Guy.'

That drew his eyes to her hand, and foolishly she covered her bracelet with her right hand. His eyes travelled up to her face and to her dismay her cheeks flooded with colour.

'Is that new? Who gave it to you?'

'It's just a – trinket,' Lesley said.

'Who gave it to you?'

'Does it matter? Do we have to digress? It's just a birthday gift, and if you must know it was from Grenville Garrison.'

'The doctor who's looking after Jane?' He was shocked and incredulous. 'Is that what this is all about? Good lord, Lesley, you're deluding yourself if you think you've fallen in love with someone as quickly as that. No, I certainly won't take my ring back.'

'It's not that at all, Guy,' said Lesley heatedly. 'Of course I don't think I've fallen in love with Dr. Garrison.' Guy had hit on the truth and it was like a flick on a raw nerve. She knew very well it was Grenville Garrison's kisses she wanted, that in her hatred for him there had been from the beginning the seed of hatred's opposite. That seed had now sprung to life, but it was not going to do her any good.

'Well then,' said Guy, apparently convinced by her vehement denial, 'let's not be so damned hasty about everything. We've had one day together. Hang on to your ring and we'll see what happens. And now let's break up the party. I have to be on that golf course and more or less mentally alert in approximately five hours. Go to bed, Lesley, have a good sleep, and I swear you'll see it all differently in the morning.' He drew her to her feet and she let him kiss her with a feeling of resignation, and as she stood passive with his mouth against hers, she couldn't help reflecting that if her angelic looks impressed Guy, then her passionate nature didn't. He couldn't even be aware that she had a passionate nature. Only one man knew about that . . .

She regretted that she had been so weak-willed when she woke in the morning. She had let Guy more or less strong-arm her into keeping up the pretence of their engagement. If he were really in love with her, then she sympathized with him, but she didn't think he was.

She had just finished washing up after a mid-morning snack that could scarcely be called breakfast when she heard the front door open. She wondered if it could be Emma Burke and went quickly into the entrance hall to make her presence known. She saw a mature-looking girl, taller than she was, with tumbled brown hair, full lips, rich colouring, and large treacle brown eyes that had dark shadows under them. She wore a red cotton tank top, white jeans and red thongs, and Lesley's immediate thought was that her name did not suit here at all. She had never pictured Emma Burke looking anything in the least like this. Voluptuous was a word she couldn't avoid.

'Hello!' said the other girl brightly. 'It's Lesley, isn't it? Sorry to break in on you – I'm after something to wear to a patio party that's come up.' Her smile was friendly, but her golden brown eyes made a pretty thorough assessment of Lesley in the apricot-coloured dress that Grenville Garrison had once called 'orange'. 'Where's Guy?'

'Playing golf,' said Lesley, and added with a smiling grimace, 'Business!'

'I know. But he will insist on being ambitious, so he

must be forgiven. Am I interrupting you?'

'No – I'm not doing a thing.'

'Then come in with me while I root out this party gear and we'll have a natter.'

Lesley sat on the divan that was her bed and Emma proceeded to root out – or in other words to take down from the built-in wardrobe – a long cotton dress, intricately tie-dyed in vermilion, tan and black.

'I owe you an apology, Lesley – or an explanation at the least,' she said as she laid the dress on the bed and began to fold it carefully. 'I suppose Guy told you that the hospital rang his number trying to get in touch with you? He was out – with me, as a matter of fact, and Douglas Potter took the call and made a bit of a boo-boo.' She left the dress and sat on the edge of her bed looking at Lesley ruefully. 'He said that Guy was out with his girl-friend.'

Lesley thought to herself, 'Douglas would say that.' It was no boo-boo – it was deliberate. But if Emma knew that, she was not giving him away.

'Well, I thought the best thing to do was to ring back just as though I were you. I know what country towns are for gossip – I was brought up in one – and I didn't want to give anyone a chance to say that your fiancé had been taking another girl out, and putting a wrong construction on it.'

She paused and Lesley said politely, 'It was kind of you to think of that.'

'Well, I meant to be helpful,' said Emma. 'But I made a boo-boo myself, I went and gave my own name. However, I just said Miss Burke, which was fortunate. I could hardly change it once I'd said it, but I hoped the doctor would take it for an error on the part of the telephonist. Did it turn out that way?'

'More or less,' said Lesley. It was over and done with now, and there was no point in telling Emma, who had been so well-intentioned, that it had started her off very much on the wrong foot with Grenville Garrison.

'Good. I was sure you'd want to go down even though you'd never even seen your little niece and Guy said you weren't close to your sister. Hadn't you been separated since you were ten or thereabouts? Still, blood is thicker than water, or so I've been told. I'm an only child myself.' She lay back on the bed, her hands clasped behind her head. 'And just to get the record straight, Lesley – about my friendship with Guy – of course he missed you and of course you wouldn't expect him to live like a monk. It just happened that we suited each other to a T. As companions,' she added. 'Guy was engaged – and mad about you. And I'm afraid I'm more interested in my career than marriage. Always have been. Marriage isn't my idea of life – dishes and household shopping and babies and so on. So one way and another we had a lot of fun together, and I just hope you don't mind.' She turned her head sideways and looked at Lesley. '*Do* you mind? I really hope not. I'd somehow pictured you rather more – sophisticated, from what Guy said.'

'I don't mind at all,' said Lesley. She wondered if she

should confide in Emma but decided she had better get things straightened out with Guy first. She said instead, 'You must have a fascinating career. You're a fashion artist, aren't you? It sounds interesting.'

'Oh yes, I have a good life. I like my work and I like my friends. I burn the candle at both ends rather too often, but when it begins to show I can shut myself up with a pile of discs, set the record player going and pass out on the bed for as long as I like. Advantage of being a bachelor girl. You can please yourself what you do – what music you listen to, whether you eat or not, any number of things. Matter of fact, I'm planning on a complete transplant soon. Time for a change.' She smiled artlessly. 'I'm off to Perth in Western Australia. That's the place for up and coming people. I've been in this particular neck of the woods too long. I need a new job, a new flat to decorate, new friends – new everything.'

Was she opting out because she had fallen in love with Guy? Lesley wished she could ask, but doubted whether she would get a truthful answer if it were so. She thought Emma was basically a nice girl, though she was not quite her type. She would not want to steal other girls' boy-friends, and she had most certainly not set out to steal Guy. But it could be as Douglas had said. The charms of a career can pale once one falls in love . . .

'Anyway, that's enough about me,' said Emma, sitting up suddenly. 'And I've been so busy talking about myself I haven't said how sorry I am about the accident. As a matter of fact, I once knew Tony Jarmyn quite well, both of us being involved in commercial art. When we were both freelancing we met several times in various magazine offices and in the art departments of some of the big advertising agencies. That was before he went abroad. I'm afraid I was the one who introduced him to Lois James – she was my flatmate for a time.'

'Lois James?' said Lesley. The name meant nothing to her.

'Didn't your sister tell you about her? I'm sorry – I should have kept my big mouth shut. I thought you were bound to know there was someone else.'

Lesley shook her head. Poor Linda! Here was another trial she had had to bear.

'Oh well, it can't do any harm to tell you now ... Lois was the giddiest of girls – just the sort Tony always got a kick out of. No one could help liking Tony in a way, but let's face it – he was about the worst marriage bet on the market. Your sister certainly didn't make a good investment in him, did she?'

'No,' said Lesley. She had reached that conclusion long ago.

'I guess Lois was more his type. She was a mad girl when I first met her – just out from England and looking for somewhere to live. She shared my flat for a few months, but she was too wild even for me, and I'm not highly shockable. I soon discovered I couldn't live with her. I've kept more or less in touch with her on and off, and I knew that she and Tony had a pretty intense affair. Maybe they quarrelled, I don't know, then he went to England and when he came back he was married. Lois shot off to Melbourne, but somehow or other they began seeing each other again.'

Lesley felt her heart skip a beat. Poor Linda! She had certainly had troubles. She wondered if Tony had been with Lois when he was away from the Cremorne flat.

'As a matter of fact,' said Emma, 'she was in Sydney not so long ago and she claimed that Tony had decided to leave his wife and take up with her again, but that could have been mere wishful thinking. At any rate, it didn't work out that way. Well, she'll get over it, you can be sure Tony wasn't the only man in her life. I'll hear from her again one of these days and she'll have lunch . . . How long are you staying, by the way?'

'I'm not sure,' said Lesley. She hadn't worked that out for herself yet.

'Stay as long as it suits you. It won't put me out. I'll be home pretty late tonight, but I'll probably see you in the morning, huh?'

'Probably,' said Lesley.

'Enjoy yourself.' Emma grabbed up her carefully folded dress and was gone.

out in it, but Tony would be away for days at a time.
He didn't want me with him, and he didn't want Jane.
I don't know what I expected to come of it. I was

CHAPTER EIGHT

It was three o'clock when Guy came back from his game of golf. He came straight to Emma's flat and threw himself down on the sofa and closed his eyes.

'I'm absolutely pooped, Lesley. Will I be in the dog box if I go to sleep and leave you to your own devices?'

'Not at all,' said Lesley. She stood looking down at him with very mixed feelings – the man she had come out from England to marry. His appearance, his language, his ways were all strange to her. She just didn't belong in his life at all. She wondered how many times he had come to this flat after a game of golf – business golf – on a Sunday morning saying he was 'pooped' and collapsing on Emma Burke's sofa. Maybe never. She didn't know now and she probably never would. To ask would make her sound jealous when she was not jealous at all – not even if Guy and Emma were madly in love.

She went to the window and looked out over the harbour, and it seemed incredible that two days earlier she had stood here with Grenville Garrison. She had made coffee for him, she had insisted that Guy's friendship with Emma was platonic. And then he had kissed her – not because he found her irresistibly attractive, but simply to prove to her that she was 'susceptible'. He had certainly proved that – and much more. He had proved to her that the physical attraction she had uneasily acknowledged to herself on her birthday had deep roots that went through to the core of her being.

She sighed and moved a little and Guy said, 'What are you thinking about, Lesley?' She looked round from the window and his eyes were open, wary, vaguely inimical. 'Not of me, I'm willing to bet.'

Well, he was the other side of the coin. Mentally she flipped it over and said with decision, 'Guy, I'm going to give you back your ring. It's going to happen, so it might as well happen now.'

He didn't move, he simply lay on his back staring at her across the room, his eyes narrowed.

He asked, 'What's changed?'

'Work it out for yourself,' said Lesley after a moment. 'We just don't – click – any more. I know I've disappointed you. I don't come up to that bright and shining image you've been holding out for inspection. I'm not putting all the blame on you,' she added quickly. 'We just don't seem to have any real point of contact any more. I suppose it's understandable enough. You've built a life here that I've never been part of.' She stopped suddenly. She was protesting too much and it made her feel ridiculously guilty. But even before she had fallen in love with someone else, she had known that she and Guy were going to split up. Now it would be quite impossible for her to marry him. It would be acting a lie.

'I get it,' Guy said slowly. 'It's Emma, isn't it? What you don't seem to realize is that even if you were completely out of the picture, Emma wouldn't marry me. If you imagine that by stepping aside you're going to leave the field clear for her to leap into my arms, you couldn't be more wrong. Emma likes to be independent. She has no intention of saddling herself with a husband and a possible family.'

'Oh, I know that,' said Lesley. It struck her as significant that he said *Emma* wouldn't marry me, *Emma* does this and that. He didn't say, Even if you weren't here, *I* wouldn't marry Emma. It was illuminating. 'Dishes and shopping and babies – Emma is a career girl . . . I suppose she has some really terrific job teed up for herself in Perth,' she added thoughtfully.

'In *Perth*? What in heaven's name are you talking about? Have you seen Emma – talked to her?'

'Yes. She came in this morning for something she needed, and we had a long talk. She told me that she's decided to tear up her roots and go to Western Australia.'

'I don't believe it,' said Guy flatly. He sat up and put his feet on the floor and looked at Lesley almost angrily – as if it were her fault that this thing, unknown to him, were happening. It was, if he only knew it, a very revealing action, a very revealing look. 'If Emma were going to Perth she'd have told me. We happen to be very good friends.'

'You *were* very good friends,' said Lesley mildly.

'But I don't think that Emma is interested in being good friends with you any longer, Guy.'

'What do you mean? What have you been saying to her?'

'Nothing,' said Lesley. 'And she hasn't a clue that you and I are breaking up. It didn't seem fair to tell her that before it was definite between us.'

He stood up restlessly, walked across the room and found a packet of cigarettes, lit one. 'And what are *your* plans? Or are they a secret from me too?'

'I'll go back down the coast,' said Lesley.

'You won't be able to adopt that kid if you're on your own,' he warned. 'You're fighting a lost cause there in any case.'

'I'm afraid you're right. But at least I can see what sort of people she will be going to – that she will go to a happy home, to people Linda would like.'

A silence fell between them. Guy threw himself down on the sofa again and smoked, his eyes half closed. Lesley didn't know what he was thinking about, but she rather suspected that her revelation about Emma had shaken him considerably. As for herself, she had said she would go back to Balgola Bay, and this she both longed for and dreaded. To see Grenville again, feeling as she now did about him, was not going to be easy, particularly when his opinion of her was so low. He must dislike her quite intensely. She recalled his parting words to her – 'I hope our relationship – as you call it – has reached its end. I shall certainly not take you back to Balgola Bay.' Hardly propitious, hardly encouraging to a girl who had been stupid and unrealistic enough to fall in love with him . . .

The telephone rang sharply, and when Guy didn't move to answer it, she did so. After all, it was Emma's flat, not his.

She knew the voice at once. Cold and imperious – and yet her heart seemed to turn over, her throat went dry. 'Is that you, Miss Brooke? I'm leaving shortly to go back down the south coast . . . Are you there?'

'Yes – yes, I'm here,' she stammered. 'I—'

'I don't imagine you're planning to return, but I promised – some time before you suggested I should mind my own business, if I remember rightly – that I'd let you know when I was leaving.'

Freezing, sardonic, and her heart despaired. It was sheer madness to love him, to let his very voice do this to her. She felt as helpless as some character in A Midsummer Night's Dream who had been put under a spell. Her love-sickness was as illogical as that . . .

She said, and was amazed at her own coolness, 'It's very kind of you to keep your promise under the circumstances, Dr. Garrison. As a matter of fact, I *am* going back to Balgola, but I don't suppose you have a spare seat in your car for me.'

A long silence. Then – 'I shall be at Kirribilli in roughly half an hour. If that gives you sufficient time, then you're welcome to come with me.'

'I'll be ready,' said Lesley, her voice shaking a little.

'Till then, Miss Brooke,' he said briefly, and hung up.

'So you're going,' Guy said. 'When?'

'In half an hour.' She slipped the sapphire ring off her finger and put it on the coffee table near the ash tray. She wished very much that she and Guy could part amicably, but that was an unreasonable hope. He had simply not made up his mind he was ready to let her go. She asked futilely, 'Guy, do you honestly think we should try again – see if we can make a go of it?'

'Not with you feeling as you do – my God, no !'

'You won't admit that you share my feelings?'

He frowned, blew out a cloud of smoke and looked over at her briefly. 'Lesley, maybe you don't know it, but you're a beautiful girl. Just looking at you is bound to do something to any healthy male. But I'll admit that your two years in purdah have done something to you. You weren't what I'd call the life of the party yesterday.'

She coloured. 'I know. I'm sorry you were disappointed, but that's the whole thing. I was never an extrovert. I think you're confusing me with Emma ... But now I must pack.'

'By all means,' he said.

So they were to part on cool terms, she thought resignedly. As if they had quarrelled. Yet wasn't it more adult to look at it the way she was doing? Or was she being selfish?

She packed, folded the bedclothes, replaced the cushions on the divan. She wrote a note to Emma in which she told her that she and Guy had decided they had drifted too far apart to go on with their engagement. She tidied her ashy hair, attended to her make-up and took her bags through to the sitting-room. Guy was sound asleep and she made a rueful face. Well, at least it was a comfort to know that he wasn't racked by misery. Her engagement ring was still where she had left it, and if he didn't see it then Emma would. Her finger felt strangely bare, but she had a strong feeling of release. However, after a second's thought she opened her handbag and took out a small case that held a pretty dress ring, and slipped it on her finger. She didn't want Grenville Garrison to know what had happened.

She said below her breath, 'Good-bye, Guy – and I wish you happiness.' Then she carried her luggage out to the elevator and went down to the street.

Grenville's car pulled up no more than two minutes later. The very sight of him caused her a sharp pang of delight, followed quickly by its converse, despair. Dark, suave, unsmiling, completely indifferent to her, though his eyebrows rose to see her standing on the pavement alone. She didn't offer any explanation, but said over-brightly, 'I'm ready, you see.'

He was silent as they started the long drive, minding his own business as she had importuned him to do. For her part, she sat beside him acutely aware of the magnetism of his physical presence, acutely aware of his complete personal withdrawal from her. There had been an almost pleasant truce between them on the journey north – he had been kindly, indulgent, point-ing out birds, plants, places that she did not know. Now the truce was over and she, who had learned too forc-ibly the meaning of her physical response to his kisses, was relegated once more to the role of foe. She won-dered if things would have been any different had Emma Burke, with the best of intentions, not caused Grenville to see Lesley from the beginning as a girl too caught up in her own love life to find time to visit her niece.

But that was to forget one basic and inescapable fact. His love belonged still to his tragically drowned young wife, and apparently always would.

When finally he spoke to her it was to ask in a pol-itely conversational way – and not as if he were in the least interested, which of course he was not – 'Did you have a pleasant week-end, Miss Brooke?'

'Yes, thank you,' she said stiffly. And then, unable to keep back the words, 'A very frivolous one, of course.'

She saw the corner of his mouth tilt, but he said nothing. She supposed he must at least be wondering what understanding she had come to with Guy – not because he was interested in her, but because it affected Jane's future. But he didn't ask, and she didn't offer any information.

At Kiama, a small town set amongst rolling green coastal hills, they stopped for a meal at a hotel, and it was impossible to sustain the complete silence into which they had fallen. As they ate, he looked across at her frowningly, his dark eyes unreadable.

'I don't wish to pry into your private life, Miss Brooke – heaven forbid – but as I encouraged you to visit Sydney with a specific purpose in mind, I should like to know if Jane is to have a home with you.'

Lesley looked back at him, and swallowed nervously. To say no was so final. Yet even if she didn't admit to it now, she would have to do so very soon. Then very soon would do, she told herself despairingly. After all, to stay long at Balgola Bay now that Grenville was so excruciatingly cool towards her would be sheer self-torture. The wise thing to do was to tell the truth, to face up to it, to surrender Jane and to go away somewhere where she could start a new life and forget him. But in spite of it all, she said weakly, 'I – I don't know.' And later she was glad she had.

His glance shifted to her left hand at the same moment as she moved it into her lap. At least he must have seen that there was a ring on her finger.

Somewhat to her surprise, he didn't follow up with the questions she dreaded. Instead, he asked her casually, 'Did you go to Cremorne?'

'Yes,' she said eagerly, relieved to have escaped without further questioning. 'Yes, I went to the flats where Linda used to live and talked to the landlady there.'

He gave her a slow burning look. 'At the risk of being told to mind my own business – I hope you don't regret it?'

'No, I don't,' said Lesley. 'I didn't hear the sort of thing people down the coast are saying. The landlady liked my sister. She was very nice and very helpful.'

'I'm glad,' he said, and Lesley knew exactly what he meant. He meant that Mrs. Fairweather had been polite and kind to Linda's sister, and that was all. She said exasperatedly, 'I'm glad too. And I believed what she told me. She didn't pretend for a minute that everything was wonderful. Linda had lots of troubles, they were in debt, Tony was – was hard to get on with. But just the same, I could *see* my sister when Mrs. Fairweather talked about her. I can't picture her at all when – when I hear things like I did at Balgola Bay. So I'd just like to know why such things are said. Even *you* believe them – I know that perfectly well, and I should like to know why.'

'Very well. If you must know,' he said after a long moment, 'both your sister and her husband had a high percentage of alcohol in their blood.' He said it bluntly, matter-of-factly. 'We don't know which of them was driving, but neither one of them should have been doing so. What happened happened because they'd been doing some very solid drinking. As far as your sister's concerned, you insist she was not like that. Very well. I must believe you. But even the best of us slips up now and again – a celebration, a bad disappointment – who knows what starts it. You'll just have to think of it that way, Lesley, if you will keep prying. Scientific facts can't be denied, I'm afraid.'

Scientific facts. Suddenly, Lesley's mind was frenziedly busy. Of course! she was exclaiming inwardly. Of course! She wondered how she could have been so blind for so long. *Of course* that girl in the car hadn't been Linda at all! It was Lois James – it had to be! It would explain everything that had puzzled her, everything. The girl the publican had known as Mrs. Jarmyn – that had been Lois James too. She was English – Emma had said so – and she was surely what could be called 'quite a girl'. Lois James was the girl described in the newspaper reports, the beautiful blonde (she *must* have been a blonde!) – the girl people like Mrs. Nelson gossiped about.

Lesley had gone quite white with the shock of her discovery, and Grenville, glancing across at her as she made no comment on his remarks, asked her sharply, 'Are you all right, Lesley?'

'Perfectly all right.' Her thoughts raced ahead. Then Linda – Linda must be somewhere. But where? And why? And how was she going to find her?

She knew now that she could not let Jane go to Judy Barnett or to anybody. She must hold on to her until she had solved the riddle of Linda's disappearance, no matter what lies she had to tell to do so. But where did she begin? To whom could she turn? She wished that Grenville would help her – but he would think her idea fantastic, that she was obsessed. And if she went to the police they would think she was a crackpot and treat her accordingly. She had to find out something definite – get hold of some positive piece of information before she took anyone into her confidence.

Meanwhile Grenville mustn't know that she had broken off her engagement to Guy. She was going to have to make him think that she believed she had almost won Guy over, no matter by what means.

For the rest of the journey down the coast, her excitement mounted. She forgave Grenville. He was right about that girl in the car — he wasn't judging her on hearsay or on wacky newspaper reports or on gossip, but on scientific facts. And she realized now that he had been considerate of her feelings. He had tried to protect her from finding out the things she had found out because he had known the truth. And now, in making excuses for 'Linda' — his very truthfulness, the scientific fact that there was alcohol in the blood — had convinced Lesley utterly and finally that the drowned girl was not Linda.

Hope took the place of despondency and now she was silent for a different reason, as her mind went over and over the problem though it got her nowhere.

It was too late when they reached Balgola Bay for her to go to see Jane. She told Grenville when he let her out of the car at Leura House, 'It will be all right about Jane. I don't want you to imagine you'll have to introduce me to Judy Barnett.' He gave her a smile that seemed to say he was sorry for her, and she turned away and went quickly inside.

Coming back here was in a way like coming home. She had her old room, there were two new faces at breakfast in the morning, and afterwards, Gilly told her, 'You look rested, Lesley. Your trip to Sydney's done you good. Everything all right with your fiancé?'

'Yes,' said Lesley, hating to tell the lie. She was wearing her dress ring, but it wasn't a very good substitute for the sapphire and she was constantly making an effort to hide it.

Jane was flourishing. She was going ahead in leaps and bounds and Lesley was allowed to take her into the hospital garden to enjoy the sunshine. Nurse Warren told her, 'She'll have you on your toes when she really gets going. You won't have a minute to call your own, she'll be into everything.'

Jane was pleased to see Lesley and her little pinched face looked brighter and even the tiniest bit plumper. She was going to be a sweet child when she was strong enough to toddle about again.

Lesley's mind was busy with a possible course of action to prove her theory, and she was looking for a starting place. That night she joined Gilly in the sitting-room when everyone else was either out or had gone to bed. The older woman was mending a minute pair of overalls that had a large tear in the seat and the radio provided a soft background of classical music.

'Well,' said Gilly, suddenly looking across at Lesley who was leaning back silent and thoughtful in her chair, 'are you going to tell me what you did in Sydney? What you plan for Jane?'

Lesley moved guiltily and shifted her left hand out of sight. 'There's nothing definite to tell you yet. I'm still — negotiating. But you tell me something, Gilly — about my sister.'

'Such as what?' Gilly gave her a sharp look. 'I didn't

know your sister, Lesley.'

'But you hear things – people gossip—'

'I don't pass on gossip.'

'This time I wish you would. I want to hear anything you can think of.'

'I can't think of anything.'

'You must have heard talk,' persisted Lesley. 'Please – even if you think I won't like it. I know,' she added, 'that they'd been drinking – that it was scientifically proven.'

'Who in the world told you that?' Sister Gilbert put her mending aside and her eyes looked angry.

'Grenville.'

'What's he thinking of? There was no need for you to know.'

'It's better that I should know – that I should face the facts. Besides,' Lesley added, 'he explained that it was probably just a celebration or something – everyone slips up sometimes. So what about the motel?' she asked, groping in her mind. Mrs. Nelson had said something about a motel.

'The Whistling Duck? They were booked in, but they didn't stay.'

'I wonder why not?'

Gilly picked up her sewing again. 'I don't know. You must know that there were debts, Lesley. People say the car wasn't paid for – that sort of thing. It wouldn't have been your sister's fault, she just didn't make a good marriage. Maybe love made up for it. Women marry gamblers, layabouts – all sorts of people, though I'm not saying your brother-in-law was any of those – and sometimes they forgive everything because of love. It's better not to worry about these things, it's all over and talk often does more harm than good.'

Lesley nodded. She wondered if she should confide in Gilly but decided against it. 'Still, I'd like to get to the Whistling Duck. It's near Merrigal, isn't it? Is there a bus?'

Gilly gave her a resigned look. 'If you're so determined to go – though why, I can't think – Grenville will be driving across tomorrow. He has to see little Sally Tressider and Ian wants him to take a look at that girl they've taken in. If you see him in the morning you could ask him to take you along – though I doubt if he will.'

Lesley doubted it too, but she was determined to go and she was not leaving it to chance. She just might miss Grenville in the morning. She thought about it silently for a couple of minutes – if she rang him he would make some excuse, put her off, or even refuse point blank. But if she went to his house – she could make him say yes, she was sure of it.

It was a good twenty minutes' walk to where he lived in the green hills behind the town. Lesley had never been there, it was dark, but there was a moon and she was determined. She knew that something beyond her rather spurious reasoning made her go to his house. Quite simply, she hungered to see him, to hear his voice, to suffer his coldness, his anger, whatever he had for her. Anything was better than nothing. . .

Shock ripped through her like a sword and left her trembling when she saw a woman come down the steps from the lighted verandah and walk through the garden towards her. She stood, her knuckles white, gripping the gatepost. She would have turned and run if she could, but her legs refused to carry her. So there was a woman in his life. Jealousy burned in her nauseatingly and painfully. 'You *idiot*, Lesley!'

And then – the woman was middle-aged, even elderly, a homely, agreeable-looking woman who stopped and asked her, 'Were you wanting the doctor, dear? He's in the sitting-room – I've just left him with a pot of coffee. Go along in – he's not busy, but even if he were he'd want you to disturb him if it's important.'

'Thank you,' breathed Lesley. 'I'll go in. You're—'

'Mrs. Neale, the housekeeper, dear.' She touched Lesley's arm kindly. 'Don't be afraid, love, it will be all right.'

Lesley wondered what she thought the trouble was. Her legs had recovered the power they had lost so ridiculously and she went on towards the house. The scent of red roses – there it was again! The garden was full of roses. They starred the night, their perfume mingling with that of the white jasmine flowers on the vine that climbed about the verandah posts. It was heady perfume on such a warm summer night and it gave Lesley a deep feeling of nostalgic sadness. Through the french windows she could see Grenville sitting reading by the light of a table lamp, his legs crossed, his clothing casual. She went quickly to the front door and rang the bell and in a minute he appeared and looked at her in surprise through the wire screen door.

'What is it, Lesley? Has something happened?' He pushed open the door and his dark face was concerned as his eyes sought hers and he motioned for her to come in. He wore dark cotton slacks and a cream shirt whose neck, opened half way down, revealed the dark hair on his chest. There were sandals on his bare feet and his dark hair was tumbled. She stared at him for seconds before she managed to stammer a reply, her heart beating madly.

'Nothing's happened. I – I wanted to ask you a favour.'

'To ask me a favour!' He gave a low incredulous laugh that was infinitely disturbing. 'Come along inside and let's hear what it is. I must confess I never thought you'd be asking favours of me, Lesley.' He saw her seated and stood looking down at her, hands on his lean hips. Then he asked with a tilt of his brows, 'Is it about Jane? Has Guy won the battle or has he surrendered?'

'It's nothing to do with that,' said Lesley quickly. 'I wanted to ask if I could come with you to Merrigal tomorrow.'

He frowned, and instead of answering, asked her, 'Would you like some coffee? There's plenty in the pot – it's just a matter of fetching another cup.'

'Thank you,' she accepted. While he was gone, she looked about her at the long beautiful room. There was a small piano, a writing desk; there were two bowls of red roses – surely his favourite flower! – and there were two bookcases. He had been reading a medical journal when she interrupted him, she saw. The cushions on the couch were flattened, and the room looked lived in yet lonely. Its colours were a soft water green, warm ivory and dull rose. Whose taste? she wondered.

When he came back he poured coffee for her and another cup for himself and sat down on the couch again, by the table lamp. It shone on his face with a soft warm light that dramatized his exceedingly good looks, and made her heart contract with a physical pleasure that was mixed with pain. She marvelled that he was taking his time like this, that he didn't say a simple yes or no and get rid of her.

'Now tell me why you want to go to Merrigal. I don't imagine it's just for the joy ride or for the pleasure of my company.'

'No,' said Lesley, her lashes falling before his quizzical glance. 'More – investigations.' She forced herself to look up and managed a rueful smile.

He moved slightly. 'When you look at me like that, you're saying a very pretty please indeed, and a far from impersonal one,' he said sardonically. 'Is it – deliberate?'

She bit her lip. Another accusation of provocation? Yet hadn't she told herself that by coming here in person she could persuade him? Colouring, she said,

'Not at all. But I know you will advise me not to go.'

'You're quite right,' he said flatly. 'I thought I'd indicated pretty clearly what the facts are. You've nothing to gain by going to the Whistling Duck. I presume that's what you intend? Just what is all this about, Lesley? In other circumstances I might suspect you of throwing yourself at me – coming here, asking for rides— As it is, I know damned well you don't want even the beginning of a personal relationship with me. Yet while you tell me one minute to mind my own business, the next you're begging me to do you a favour – to cart you about the countryside as if we were the best of friends.'

'I know we're not that,' said Lesley, her voice low. 'I know you dislike me intensely – and most things about me. But I can't help what you think – I must go to the Whistling Duck.'

He looked exasperated. 'You're never satisfied, are you? You just can't let well alone. Can't you accept the explanation I offered you the other day? Nobody's perfect, Lesley, if that's what you're intent on proving. Nobody.'

She met his eyes and saw somewhere at the back of them a darkness and a compassion that made her heart lurch.

'What *do* you want to prove?' he asked gently.

She drew a deep breath. 'That it was not Linda.' It had to be said to someone, and she somehow couldn't stop herself from confessing it to this man with whom she was in love.

He put down his cup and she could see he was at the end of his patience. 'For God's sake, why would it not be Linda?'

'Because Linda was not like that.'

'My God,' he said below his breath. Then harshly, 'Look, Lesley, I've told you before that people change. I'll be more specific.' He reached for a cigarette and lit it, and Lesley thought his hand shook slightly. 'I'm going to tell you something – and I hope it will be for your good, that it will widen your understanding of human nature. Something that I've never told to another living person. Then perhaps you will know what I mean when I say that people can change, and you will learn to accept as I have done and not spend useless hours looking for perfection where it doesn't exist – even to the extent of trying to wipe out facts when you can't prove them wrong.' He leaned back and looked at her in the lamplight and his eyes had a hard glitter in them that frightened her a little. 'Has anyone ever told you that I was once married, that I lost my wife in a drowning accident?'

She nodded.

'Well, it was not an accident. Alison drowned herself. She walked into the sea intending never to come out again.'

Lesley stared at him, shocked. The girl he had loved so devotedly had drowned herself! It was incredible. She asked huskily, 'How could you know? Unless she told you she was going to do it—'

'She didn't tell me, but I know. And it happened

because she had changed drastically from the lovely young girl I married. We didn't know each other very well when we fell in love and rushed into marriage. It wasn't till afterwards that I discovered she didn't want children. More than that, she was fanatically afraid of having a child. And as fate would have it, she became pregnant in less than three months. For her it was a disaster. She was really terrified, and yet she wouldn't have her pregnancy terminated – that was another of her irrational fears. I told myself that it would be different once the baby was born – that her maternal instinct would save the situation – but it wasn't to be as simple as that. The baby was born, but he lived only four days, and Alison became obsessed with feelings of guilt. She couldn't sleep, she suffered from blinding headaches, she wouldn't listen to anything I tried to tell her. In fact, she couldn't bear me near her, I couldn't touch her. We became strangers, there was no love left between us.' He looked down at his cigarette and tapped ash from it. 'I took her to Sydney to see a psychiatrist, but she wouldn't co-operate. She just didn't want to take up normal life again. She was drowned soon after we came home. It was supposed to be an accident – she had been washed off the rocks by a freak wave. But I know quite surely that she drowned herself.'

'But why? When you were trying to help her – when you understood – You *can't* know,' said Lesley.

'I can and I do. Understanding wasn't enough. If we'd still loved one another it might have been different, I don't know. But our marriage was over, there was nothing of it left. She didn't want to live. Yet only a year before she'd been a gay and happy girl . . . And that's the point of this story, Lesley. People can change, and it's not necessarily their fault. It just happens that way. It's something you have to learn to live with. It may be hard, bitter, but it has to be done. Do you think my memories give me anything but pain?'

She looked at him helplessly and shook her head. She felt an immense compassion for him, and she wondered why he had told her all this. It didn't make her feel any different about Linda. There was Mrs. Fairweather's 'evidence' – there was the fact that Tony had been having an affair with another woman. But now was hardly the time to tell Grenville these things. The atmosphere in the lamplit room had become oddly tense. All he had told her was churning around in her mind, and at the back of it all she was aware that the mystique of his being a man dedicated to his work and still in love with the memory of his dead wife was a false one. Dedicated to his work, yes, but surely a man who was still capable of falling in love, even though he must have grown wary of personal entanglements after his deeply unhappy experience . . .

She said unsteadily, 'Thank you for trying to be helpful, Grenville, but I must go to Merrigal. I still don't believe that woman was Linda.' His name had slipped out for the first time, and it added to the strange sense of intimacy in the room. He was aware of it too, but when he said, 'So be it, Lesley,' and they both got to their feet he didn't attempt to detain her. The room was full of danger – they had reached a curious point where something drastic was going to happen in another moment. And before it could happen, Grenville was intent on making a move, in getting Lesley out of the house, in bringing matters down to earth.

'I'll drive you home,' he said, and now his voice was aloof. She wondered if he regretted having confided in her.

CHAPTER NINE

SHE explained her belief to him the next afternoon as they drove to Merrigal. She was aware of a subtle change in their relationship, but she did not know exactly what the change was. The fact that he was after all not in love with a memory could have no personal significance for her . . . She felt she owed it to him to tell him why she believed what she did about Linda. He had entrusted her with a story, he was taking her to the motel against his own inclinations.

It was a gloriously sunny day, but there was a breeze from the sea and the drive was extremely pleasant, along a road that wandered through bushland, now within sight of the sea, now going into the hills. Merrigal was some miles inland, and as they drove, Lesley said diffidently, 'I know you think it's a crazy idea I have about Linda—'

'Crazy?' He sent her an oblique smile that set her senses spinning. 'That's an understatement, Lesley. It's sheer unadulterated wishful thinking on your part. I'm afraid that sums it up.'

'And I'm afraid it doesn't,' contradicted Lesley. 'I have very good grounds for my theory.'

'Let's hear them then.'

'You might be bored.'

'You might have been bored by the long and obviously useless tale I served up to you last night,' he said dryly. 'So let's have it.'

'Very well, then.' She paused, wondering where to begin, then plunged in. 'Linda was always a gentle sort of a girl – she loved children and she had a kind heart. That's the sort of girl Mrs. Fairweather was talking about at Cremorne. It's not the sort of girl the newspapers or Mr. Prescott talked about – a beautiful blonde, when she wasn't even a blonde, quite a girl – oh, I was sick to death of hearing things like that, things that didn't fit Linda's character at all.'

'So?' he asked sceptically as she paused.

'So then Emma Burke told me about this girl Tony was having an affair with, and she was just the sort of girl the man at the Pacific Hotel talked about. Exactly that sort. And when you told me it was true that she'd been drinking, suddenly I realized that the girl with Tony was Lois James and not Linda. Don't you see? It fits so perfectly. The only problem is – where is Linda? What's happened to her?'

'That certainly *would* appear to pose a problem,' he said seriously enough. 'But there's one other thing, Lesley – and I'm afraid it completely upsets your theory. And that is the child's presence in the car. If Tony Jarmyn was going away with another woman, they'd hardly have taken Jane along with them too, would they?'

Lesley felt knocked completely flat. She was staggered by her own stupidity. Of course they would not have taken Jane with them – even if they had wanted to, Linda would not have allowed it. And where did that leave her? With the unpalatable fact that her theory was quite ridiculous. For a second she hated Grenville for so cruelly destroying her hopes, and when he put a hand lightly over hers, she drew away as though stung.

'I'm sorry about it,' he said coolly. 'But don't blame me for the collapse of your dreams ... Do you still want to go to the motel? Or will you come with me to the Tressiders'? I'm sure young Sally would be pleased to see you.'

'I'll go to the Whistling Duck,' said Lesley, her voice low. 'That's why I'm here – I didn't come along for the ride and I know you don't want to drag me about with you, paying social calls.'

Five minutes later he pulled up at a long low modern motel built in an L shape. 'There you are, Lesley,' he said briskly. 'Make your inquiries – and be rational about your wild hopes. There's a coffee bar somewhere – you might wait for me there, and I'll pick you up later.'

'Thank you,' she said. She didn't look back as he drove away, but went with a determination and confidence that she no longer really felt towards the reception office. It occurred to her that it would have made her lot much easier all along if she had happened to have a photograph of Linda, but she hadn't – Linda had sent none from Australia, not even one of Jane. She knew that she was going to have to accept Grenville's assessment of the situation finally. Something had upset Linda's personality – no matter what Mrs. Fairweather had said.

In the reception office, a smart-looking middle-aged woman greeted her brightly. 'Did you want to book in?'

'No – I just wanted to ask about some people who stayed here a few weeks ago – Mr. and Mrs. Jarmyn,' said Lesley rather listlessly.

'The Jarmyns? The couple who were drowned?'

'Yes. My sister was married to Tony Jarmyn, but I have reason to believe she was not the woman with him,' said Lesley with decision. 'I thought you might be able to help me.'

'Have you a photograph?'

'I'm afraid not.'

The woman shrugged. 'Then the police would be the best people to go to.'

'I suppose so. But – but could you just tell me what Mrs. Jarmyn looked like?'

'Well, let's see. She was a blonde – dyed her hair, I should think, it didn't look natural – a little taller than you, more flesh on her bones, attractive—' She paused. 'That's about all I can remember. Does it help?'

It didn't really, and Lesley's heart sank. Such a woman could quite well have been Linda. She could have bleached her hair – even while Mrs. Fairweather was away. Her hopes had more or less died, but she persisted, 'Is there anything else you can remember about them? Anything at all—'

'Well, I don't know. They came after dinner – they

were in a good mood. They brought their own drinks – must have, because they didn't buy anything at the bar here, and they left a few empties in their room. We went over all that with the police, anyhow. How is the kiddie, by the way? We never saw her – didn't hear a peep out of her. She must have been asleep.'

'She's almost well again,' said Lesley.

'She had a lucky escape, didn't she? My husband said neither of them should have got behind the wheel of a car after all the drink they must have tucked away. It was a shocking night too – rain coming down in buckets. We never did find out what got them on to the road in such a hurry – we didn't hear a thing in the storm. We were fairly empty that night and they were tucked away at the short end of the L.'

It was obvious that she wasn't going to get any clues here. The only thing left – and she wondered a little if it was even worth doing – was to try to get a photograph of Lois James from Emma, and it would be very lucky indeed if one happened to be available. Finally, she thanked the woman at the motel and walked slowly over to the restaurant where she sat at a table by the window and ordered coffee. She supposed it could be some time before Grenville was back, and she sipped the coffee and thought about her wonderful theory – and of how it had been so quickly destroyed. She was feeling very low-spirited when unexpectedy, Grenville's voice asked her, 'Well, Lesley, what did you unearth this time?'

She gave a start of surprise and glanced up. He was

standing beside the table and his dark eyes looked down at her enigmatically. She thought they were more searching than ever just now – they seemed to examine her own eyes very thoroughly, and at last she was compelled to drop her lashes.

'I didn't unearth anything at all,' she said honestly. 'But I still can't convince myself. I know you think I'm stupid, and stubborn, but it's because of what Mrs. Fairweather said.'

'I see . . . Have you finished your coffee? If so, then I think we'd better get back on the road.' His voice was oddly controlled and she didn't know what to make of it. He didn't seem particularly interested or concerned in the fact that she had discovered nothing, or even in her stubborn protestations. All he wanted was to get back to the car.

But once they were there he didn't start the motor immediately. He asked her, 'Was your sister at all like you, Lesley? Did she too have those smoke blue eyes?'

She felt herself flinch and her nerves began to tingle. 'We weren't very alike – except for our eyes. Jane's are the same colour. Why?'

He ignored her question. His eyes narrowed and he turned in the seat and looked at her seriously. 'Lesley, I decimated that extraordinary theory of yours a while ago, because of the child's presence in the car. I still can't account for that, but I'm not at all sure now that you aren't right.'

Her heart began to beat sickeningly fast. 'What –

what do you mean?' Her voice was a mere whisper. 'It was true what you said – Tony and Lois would never have taken Jane with them—'

'There could be some other explanation as to why she was in the car. We just don't know. But I want you to come to the Tressiders' with me. And I'm warning you, I could possibly be making a bad mistake, but I think not. I believe that young woman whom Ian Tressider is sheltering is your sister.'

Lesley felt every drop of blood drain from her face and she stared at him wordlessly.

'She's suffering from amnesia. She has light brown hair and eyes like yours and she's around thirty. There's absolutely nothing the matter with her beyond the fact that she's completely lost her memory. The police have made investigations, but she doesn't answer the description of any missing person.'

Lesley felt a mad hope surge through her. 'It's Linda – it must be – I knew I was right!'

'I hope you are.' He started up the motor and as they drove to the town he told her as much as he knew about this girl who must be Linda. She had wandered on to the dairy farm belonging to some people called Roland a few weeks before. She was weak and ill and she had a head injury and was suffering from amnesia. They got her to bed and called in a doctor who said the amnesia had probably been caused by a blow on the head combined with some sort of nervous strain. Rest and care were the main things the girl needed, and in time her memory would come back. So the Rolands undertook to look after her.

'She is all right?' Lesley quavered.

'Yes. But she's apparently been under great stress and the amnesia has persisted. Ian Tressider met her several times when he went to visit the Rolands — they're members of his church — and he decided to bring her back to Merrigal where she'd be able to live a more normal and less isolated life. Jean is a trained nurse and she and Ian both like the girl tremendously. She's very good with young Sally, apparently.'

'Linda would be,' said Lesley. 'Do you think if she saw Jane again her memory might come back?'

'It could do.'

They had reached the Tressiders' home now and Lesley's two hands were gripping each other and she was biting on her lower lip to keep it steady.

'Take it easy now, Lesley,' Grenville told her as they went up the steps together. The front door was open and they went straight in. Jean Tressider appeared from a room on the left. 'In here, Lesley,' she said quietly.

And in another second Lesley was staring across the room at her sister.

Linda was sitting in an armchair doing some embroidery — a thing she had always been good at. She raised her head as Lesley came in. Her face was thin and pale and a little sad, and for a long moment her eyes looked back at Lesley without recognition. Then slowly she got to her feet. Her embroidery and scissors fell to the floor. She held out her hands and came forward like a sleepwalker.

'Lesley!'

She said the one word and fainted dead away.

When she recovered consciousness, memory came flooding back, and presently the two sisters were left together to talk. The first thing Linda wanted to know was where Jane was, and as soon as Lesley told her she was safe at Balgola Bay, she relaxed and her thoughts went to Tony.

'He was in a bad accident,' said Lesley carefully. 'I'm afraid he's – gone, Linda.'

To her relief, Linda took the news quietly, though she put her face in her hands and shed a few tears. Then – 'And Lois James?'

Lois James! So Lesley's deductions had been quite right. 'She was drowned too.'

After that, Linda wanted to talk, to tell Lesley the story not only of that night but of her disastrous marriage that went from bad to worse – the debts, Tony's extravagance, his irritation that they were so hamstrung by the baby. That was why he had started to go out by himself, and then, when he met up again with Lois James whom he had known before, things got really out of hand.

'I just never had any money – he didn't seem to care. And yet he was earning all we needed and more. We owed rent and electricity and the chemist, and he kept buying the most extravagant and unnecessary things. We even had a motor cabin cruiser once! I never went out in it, but Tony would be away for days at a time. He didn't want me with him, and he didn't want Jane. I don't know what happened to it eventually – I suppose he sold it. Then he told me he was going to leave me. It was terrible, Lesley – I had loved him so much and I couldn't believe it had all ended in nothing. I kept praying it would all come back again. I was half out of my mind. I wrote to you to ask you to help me—'

'I remember,' said Lesley. 'But I didn't know what it was all about.'

'I shouldn't have fought against it,' said Linda. 'I should have given him up – let them go.' She leaned back in the couch and stared ahead of her. 'It all came to a head quite suddenly. Tony was away and I'd taken Jane out for a walk one afternoon. When I came home, he was there. He'd packed up all his things and was loading them into the car. I asked where he was going. He said he was picking up Lois and they were going to Melbourne, that they'd stop overnight in a motel in Merrigal. He seemed to take a delight in telling me all the details.' Her mouth twisted sadly. 'He said he was leaving me – that we were through for good. I should have accepted it, it was a hopeless marriage – ever since Jane was born nothing went right. But I was so alone, and I thought that once you had loved—' She broke off, her blue eyes cloudy and troubled. 'I ran inside and rang the railway to see when I could get a train. There was one at six o'clock as far as Nowra, and from there I didn't know how I'd get to

Merrigal. I really think I went a little insane – I was so determined to get him back. I reached Nowra about ten o'clock, and there was no taxi and no bus. It was raining and I started to walk with Jane all wrapped up in my raincoat. I'd had to bring her with me because the landlady was away, and anyhow I don't think I'd have left her in any case. Finally I got a lift with two girls. I told them I was on my way to visit my aunt, and they didn't seem to think it was odd that I should be carrying a small child and trying to thumb a ride. They thought it was fun.' She smiled wryly. 'Anything goes these days if you're young enough, though heaven knows I felt far from young that night. Anyhow, I was lucky with the girls and I was lucky with the motel. I chose the right one. I saw Tony's car outside one of the units when I went in. It was terribly late and it was raining again. Jane was asleep and I put her in the back of the car because my arms were aching, and anyhow I didn't want her to wake up and be frightened if we had a row. I knocked on the door of the unit and Tony opened the door, and he was absolutely furious when he saw me. I suppose he'd been drinking – I never told you before, but it was one of his weaknesses. I think – I think he must have struck me, because after that I don't remember anything at all. The next thing I knew was when I woke up in bed at the Rolands' dairy farm. I don't know how I got there. Everything was strange and my head was aching and I was frightened. It was as if all my life had been a dream and I couldn't remember any of it. You know how it is when you wake up and your dreams have vanished?'

She looked worn out now, and Lesley assured her, 'That's all in the past, Linda. I'm here now and tomorrow you'll see Jane again and in no time you'll have forgotten all this.' She was relieved that Jean Tressider came in then.

'Grenville wants to go presently, Lesley. Would you come and say hello to Sally before you go? She's had a little chill and I've had to keep her in bed.' She rested her hand lightly on Linda's shoulder as she spoke. 'I'm so happy about Linda. I often felt she reminded me of someone, but I never thought of you. Ian and I would very much like her to continue staying with us as long as she likes. Jane can come here too, of course – it's a big house.'

She smiled at Linda and it was plain to see the two women liked each other. Lesley went to see Sally and found her sitting up in bed with a puzzle book. She talked to her for a few minutes and then Grenville came to find her.

'Ready now, Lesley?'

She got up immediately and said good-bye to Sally. He told her, 'Make it a quick good-bye to your sister, will you? I've just been in to see her and that girl should go to bed. She's had a lot of excitement, but I don't think there's much to worry about in her condition.'

As they drove back to Balgola Bay Lesley told him briefly the story Linda had told her. He said, thoughtfully, 'So your hunch – your intuition – was right, Lesley. I don't suppose those other two ever knew the child was in the car. It was a most remarkable escape for her – and looks like being a happy ending all round. I rather gathered from Jean that Ian has lost his heart to your sister, but only time will tell if anything's to come of that ... There'll be a bit of business to go through with the police, by the way,' he added casually. 'The other girl will have to be identified, but I don't think that should be difficult. At all events, Ian's promised to take care of everything, and you can be sure that Linda will be shielded as much as possible from any unpleasantness.'

It was not until they had reached Balgola Bay and were driving, not up to the headland in the direction of Leura House, but into the green hills behind the town, that Lesley realized he was not taking her home.

'We shan't subject you to that yet,' he explained. 'I phoned through to Sister Gilbert while you were talking to your sister and gave her the extraordinary news, and promised I'd keep you away until the excitement had died down a litttle.' He pulled up in the drive outside his own house, and as they climbed the steps to the verandah, he remarked coolly, 'The first thing you'll want to do when we get inside is to ring your fiancé and tell him what's happened, I should imagine.'

It was just on sundown, magpies were warbling in the garden and the scent of red roses was heavy on the air. The glow of sunset added a strange hot sheen of bronze to the garden and was reflected too in Grenville's dark face as he turned at the front door to look at her. Lesley, who had not even thought of Guy, felt the colour drain from her cheeks. She was suddenly aware that for her, everything was almost over. Now there would be no further excuse for staying at Balgola Bay. She would have to make a move and it would be best to go right away where she could start again – try to forget Grenville Garrison, and perhaps some day in a barely conceivable future fall in love again.

'Well?' he said, holding the door open for her. 'It's not too early to ring, is it? Guy should be home from work now. And in all fairness, it's your move now, you know, Lesley. The cards have fallen his way this time, haven't they? You've a very tidy solution to your problem, and your marriage should get off to a flying start. I suppose you can hardly wait to get your bags packed and say good-bye.'

Lesley couldn't look at him. She said faintly, 'I'll let Guy know about Linda, of course. But we're not going to be married. I should have let you know before, but – but I didn't want you to arrange for Judy Barnett or someone to adopt Jane.' It was out now and she was glad she had told him the truth. She hadn't gone inside, and he let the wire door go and it shut with a bang. He stood looking down at her darkly.

'It's Emma Burke, is it?' he asked grimly. 'When I saw you wearing this bauble' – he reached for her left hand and indicated her dress ring accusingly – 'I took it to mean that you hadn't after all been able to "persuade" Guy – and that you were taking the most drastic means you could think of. It seems I was wrong. It's Miss Burke. I'm sorry, Lesley.'

'There's nothing to be sorry about,' said Lesley. 'And please don't blame Emma. I certainly hope that she and Guy will marry, but—'

'You hope? Isn't it a certainty, then? Isn't it why *you* and Guy are not to be married?' He gave a sudden low exclamation and took her roughly by the wrist. 'Now listen to me – I've had enough prevarications and unpalatable half-truths from you to last me a lifetime, Lesley Brooke. You started the moment we met – and I not so very long ago discovered how badly I'd misjudged you – and it seems you haven't given up yet. I want one or two straight answers from you and I want them now and willingly, or I promise you I shall force them from you by foul means.'

His eyes looked down into hers, deadly serious and glittering, though his lips were curved in a curiously gentle smile. She felt a shiver go through her.

'First of all, are you still in love with Guy Longden? Answer me – yes or no.'

'No,' she said in a whisper, her heart pounding in her breast.

'That's fine. When did it all end? When you made up that stubborn mind of yours that you must have Jane and he wouldn't agree to share you?'

She shook her head. 'When he met me at the airport. He was so different – I knew then—'

He looked at her incredulously, and now the smile

reached back into the darkness of his eyes.

'All that time ago? And yet you acted the part of an engaged girl as though your very life depended on it. I thought you were madly in love, even though Gilly, apparently more astute than I, insisted that you were not, that all was far from well. I thought that no man in his senses could wait a moment longer than he had to to take you in his arms, to make you his own. I even thought that your weariness, when first we met, was from the hours of ecstasy you'd spent in another man's arms. And how that came to rankle! If I'd known what you've just told me, I'd have—' He stopped abruptly and his eyes went to her lips, and he began to draw her towards him.

'Lesley, look at me. Are you possibly – by the remotest chance – in love with me, my passionate angel? As much in love as I am with you? Come here and let me find out for myself if it's true – if the fervour with which you answered my kisses that night on the beach is for me—'

'It is,' she breathed. 'It is!' Willingly she let him pull her into his arms and set his lips against her own. Her senses reeled, the sky tilted, she could smell red roses and the whole world was a wonderful place.

FREE!!!
Did you know . . . . . . ?

that just by mailing in the coupon below you can receive a
brand new, up-to-date "Harlequin Romance Catalogue"
listing literally hundreds of Harlequin Romances you
probably thought were out of print.

Now you can shop in your own home for novels by your
favorite Harlequin authors — the Essie Summers you
wanted to read, the Violet Winspear you missed, the Mary
Burchell you thought wasn't available anymore!

They're all listed in the "Harlequin Romance Catalogue".
And something else too — the books are listed in numerical
sequence, — so you can fill in the missing numbers in your
library.

Don't delay — mail the coupon below to us today. We'll
promptly send you the "Harlequin Romance Catalogue"

FREE!

Have You Missed Any of These
Harlequin Romances?